About the Author

June Oldham lives in Ilkley, Yorkshire, and spends
her days writing in an attic from which she can see
the m_   _ween books she h_s held w_iting
_idences, and she does workshops and readings. As
well as her books for teenagers and children, she writes
novels for adults, one of which, *Flames* (Virago), was
awarded a prize. Her leisure interests are theatre, film,
walking, conversation and listening.

June Oldham.

Praise for 'Escape'

'a powerfully told story of truth and survival.'
The Daily Telegraph
  '. . . tackles incest with grace, honesty and slill.'
The Oxford Times
  'An engrossing and deeply moving book which
offers no easy answers.' *Books for Keeps*

June
OLDHAM

Escape

Hodder
Children's
Books

a division of Hodder Headline Limited

First published in Great Britain in 1996
by Hodder Children's Books
a division of Hodder Headline Limited
338 Euston Road
London NW1 3BH

This edition published in 2002.

10 9 8 7 6 5 4

A Catalogue record for this book is available from the British Library

ISBN 0 340 68724 X

Typeset by Avon DataSet Ltd, Bidford-on-Avon, B50 4JH

Printed and bound in Great Britain by
Clays Ltd, St Ives plc

One

A slight breeze was rippling the curtains but it brought no air into the room. If she weren't asleep in ten minutes, Magdalen promised herself, she would get up and open the window wider. She rearranged her pillows, pulled the sheet straight and turned her face away from the clock. The thing was faulty, she decided; last time she had looked at it, the hands appeared to have moved back. After another doze, she would check with her watch. Meanwhile, there was a small area somewhere near her shoulder blade that itched. Unable to reach it, she thought, What's the word for the section of your back you can't get at, unless you're a contortionist? Ac-something. She tried to track it down: accost, accursed, ache, then gave up. Her father would know it; his vocabulary was phenomenal. It was probably the only thing about him she would miss. That is, if her plan succeeded. Her breath left her. By half-past ten she would know.

Somewhere in the town a church clock struck the hour. She counted the chimes: five. It was still night to most people, to those who slept at ease in their beds. Magdalen finally gave up the pretence. Standing by her window, she was reminded of the view from a plane during a night journey, the street lamps threading the valley in a beaded mesh. Perhaps he was sleepless, too, striding along the carpet in his hotel bedroom, as anxious as she was. His pride would be hurt if she didn't do well. And if she did, if . . . She gripped the edge of the window sill. If she did get good grades and she carried out her intention, she dared not imagine how he would behave. This morning there was more than her father's pride at stake.

Across the valley, the moor was fully visible, its crest a dark streak against the pale sky. The town, the moor, the house were silent. It seemed that she was the sole person in the whole country who was awake. Perhaps alive. The only sounds in this dead world were those she made and she was harshly aware of them: dressing, she heard the zip of her jeans creak as she closed it; electricity in her hair crackled through the comb; her feet on the stairs thudded. In the kitchen, the click of a spoon against the lip of the beaker rang out like a summoning bell. Usually before going to bed, checking the windows and doors, she was happy with such noises because they were entirely hers; they emphasised the fact that he was not there. But now, amplified in the quiet of an early morning, they alarmed her and she wished she were not alone.

That's pathetic, she rebuked herself. The last thing I want is him coming back.

The house was closing in upon her. She had to get out. Stuffing a packet of crisps in her pocket, she rose quickly and left the kitchen. There was a long passage from what had once been the servant quarters and as she walked down it the walls seemed to lean, making it narrower; soon there would be only a slit for her body to push through; then she must get across the hall, through the door, down the long drive to the high beech hedge which shut in the house. She had to get out, but her legs were moving too slowly. She wanted to reach the road where wide lawns ran down to the pavement. Then she would not feel constricted. She would do as she had done many times when her father was absent or still asleep. She would walk under the street lamps which rimed the grass with saffron, shone on the branches of the trees and tinselled the leaves. Away from the lamps, helped by the dawn light, she would take a path, then a flight of steps furred with moss. And when she reached the moor, she would not look at the town glowing below her; she would not even glance in the direction of this house. For a short space she would put it behind her and all that had happened in it.

'And I shall. For ever,' she told herself as she entered the hall. 'If . . .' She could not finish the sentence. The possibility of failure washed over her; it took away her strength, her feet stumbled on the thick rugs that lay scattered over the tiled floor and at the door her fingers would not pull back the bolts. So she left it and slowly, like one crippled, she returned to her room.

She could see that on the opposite side of the valley it was now full morning; thin shadows replaced the darkness under trees and walls. A tractor circled farm buildings then chugged up a track. If I don't get the grades I need, I'll think of something, Magdalen tried to encourage herself, my ingenuity isn't used up, it's only got a bit rusty while he's been away. But the prospect of failure would not leave her; it fumbled her fingers as she opened the packet of crisps. At the same moment she heard the rumble of a train, then the scrape of its brakes. It was bringing the mail. Take a grip on yourself, she ordered; you have to do better than this when you go into school, meet Gail and the rest of them, read the results pinned on the board. There were crisps on the carpet. Bending to pick them up, she dropped the rest. Anybody seeing me would say I was suffering from a touch of hysteria, she said. And immediately she was looking into her father's face.

'Do you know where that word comes from?' he had asked her. 'From the Greek *hystera* meaning the womb. It's believed to be responsible for women being unstable and overemotional, particularly without reason. Hysteria's not your style, Magdalen, is it? Neither of us wants that.'

Magdalen stared at the town below her. The street lamps had been switched off; cars moved along the main thoroughfare; vans, their lights flashing, were parked outside shops; there was the crunch of gravel on her drive, the clink of bottles and a milk float's wheeze. But Magdalen was aware of none of this, neither was she thinking of examination grades. As the hours passed, her fingers dug into the curtains, her body tensed and her cheeks flinched. She was remembering.

By the time Magdalen walked from the house, the town was busy. Conscientious shoppers were laden; the first tourists had arrived, distinguished by their meandering gait; mothers sighing for the end of the school holidays were herding offspring towards the swimming baths. The sun was out, the sky was cloudless and she was suddenly tweaked by hope. It disappeared as soon as she entered the school and saw the rest of the Sixth excited, chattering, comparing results.

'Magdalen!' Gail shouted and strode towards her. 'We were beginning to wonder where you were.'

'I've had a bad night.'

'Who hasn't? But you'd no need to worry.'

Magdalen asked, 'How have you done?' She was trying to delay approaching the noticeboard but Gail was steering her to it, saying, 'I'm all right. Manchester'll take me.'

Then she was staring at the large square print-out, dragging her eyes down the list, reading each name though she knew they were in alphabetical order and hers would be at the end. Finally she reached it and, opposite, a line of A's.

She heard, 'You've done brilliantly, Mag.' Gail's tone was affectionate, untainted by envy. 'You have to see Mr Gresham; we've all been.'

The headmaster's hand was large and slightly rough, unlike her father's. It shook hers briefly, then Mr Gresham remarked that her fingers were cold. 'You look very pale, Magdalen. You're not about to be ill?' He was nervous, checking the distance from his buzzer, and she realised he meant: 'Are you going to throw up?' because she had done that on the morning he gave out the first paper and he had moaned, 'This hasn't happened before in my whole experience.' Recovering, she had answered, 'Nor in mine.'

She heard him repeat the question and she shook her head. 'All I want to know is: will Edinburgh take me?'

'Most certainly. They have confirmed the provisional offer. I'm very pleased, Magdalen. You deserve these grades; your father has mentioned that you've been burning the midnight oil while he's been abroad.'

She nodded, not bothering to ask how her father had found out.

'I hope you'll come back to say goodbye before you begin your course. I'm sure you're looking forward to it, starting a new life.' He was still anxious, wishing he had a bowl handy. 'Now I'll let you return to the others and I want a word with members of staff. Several have come into school this morning.'

From the window of the staff room Harley Gresham watched the A level candidates walk down the drive. 'I must be growing sentimental, Melanie,' he said, addressing a younger teacher, 'but I'm sorry to see that lot go. How in the world did you and your colleagues prise those grades out of Magdalen Wilde?'

'They were what we predicted.'

'Indeed, and I confess that at the time I was astonished by your assessment.'

'I think she suddenly discovered motivation.'

'A pity she didn't do that lower down the school. She was one of those infuriating young things you know has brains but won't use them. It was a great worry to her father. As was, of course, all that running away.'

'Did she do that? I didn't know.'

'It must have been before your time. How long have you been with us? Two years? Yes, she'd disappear. She'd make for the coast, favoured Northumbria for some reason. Generally, she'd be picked up in the Bamburgh area.'

'It has beautiful sands.'

'I don't think she took her bucket and spade. I never understood why she did it. It wasn't that she was in trouble, anything of that kind, and she has a good home background. It was a terrible problem for her father; he and I would discuss it at length. He's first-rate; a devoted parent. I only wish all our pupils were as fortunate.' Mr Gresham paused. 'Good heavens! Do you know, a young chap has appeared and sat bang in the middle of the lawn as bold as brass. He's not one of ours, either.'

'No, he's with me,' Melanie said, glancing out of the window. 'I think he's suggesting he's ready to go.'

'Should I know him?' Harley Gresham asked tentatively. He was never quite sure of his ground nowadays with junior staff when it came to domestic arrangements but this fellow looked several years younger than Melanie.

'He's a cousin, staying with me for a few days. He came into school because he knows one or two of the Sixth. I'd better go.'

Outside she told Greg, 'I got the feeling that Mr Gresham thought you might be my partner.'

They laughed and he asked, 'Would that be incest?'

'No, I don't think so. Anyway, did you manage to arrange a game or was everyone too excited to think of squash?'

'They were definitely high, but I fixed up to play with Matthew and two of the girls. Also, tomorrow I'm invited to a party.'

'Where?'

'At one of the girls'. Magdalen something.'

'Magdalen Wilde.'

'Did you teach her?'

'Yes. Physics. She'll be going to Edinburgh to read medicine.'

'She seemed to have no problem about throwing a party. No one else felt up to springing it on parents at such short notice or trying to clear them out.'

'She hasn't a mother and when her father's away presumably she can please herself.'

'That's convenient.'

Gail expressed the same sentiment as she and Magdalen walked home. 'Just being able to throw a party and no hassle! What would I give to be in your shoes!'

'You must say that, on average, twice a month. It comes round more often than PMT.'

'I'd give my back teeth,' Gail declared, having decided upon the level of sacrifice, 'to have our house to myself. In ours it's such a crush and everything's so public. You can't be in the loo or the bathroom without somebody banging on the door. That's Peter mostly; he's into washing his hair. Have you noticed? When I'm going out, Mum always asks where to, and when I'll be back. It doesn't matter what I do, at least one of them knows.'

'I don't do a lot. But if I did, Dad would find out. He'll know about the party.'

'How?'

'He's got spies.'

'Oh, come on!'

'If you like, you can call them fans, but there's no difference. They report back. To be honest, I don't think they do it because they want to sneak on me. It's an excuse for keeping in touch with him. Like Mrs Dawson across the road. She's one of his fans. He collects them.'

Gail sighed. 'I wouldn't mind being collected.'

'I thought you'd say that.'

They had reached Magdalen's house. Looking down the drive, Gail said, 'That room of yours, not your bedroom, the one on the second floor, I do like it. It's a half octagon, isn't it? I always think of it as a turret.'

'I don't think about it, Gail. I just work in it.'

'Yes, you put the time in. Rather you than me. I'm glad I didn't want to read medicine. I'll have to be going. I said I'd be back at the café in time to help serve lunch. Are you at the petrol station this afternoon?'

'Yes.'

'Oh, there's something I meant to tell you, about the bloke who was with Matthew.'

'What bloke?'

'You should remember, you included him in the invitation to your party.'

'I didn't notice him.'

Gail tutted. 'He's Greg, a cousin of Miss Howkins, at art college, doing graphics and design. What I thought you'd like, Mag, is that he was off to Armley Gaol.'

'To visit or turn himself in?'

'I knew you'd ask that! I wish I had. He's going because he wants to sketch it. It's Victorian, he says, and built like a castle and he wants one for a series of illustrations, for a strip cartoon.'

'What's the story?'

'Now that question I did ask, but he shrugged, said he was thinking of some kind of fairy-tale, only modern, up to date. Relevant.'

Magdalen intoned, 'Relevant!' and they both laughed.

'Well, the Rombalds Snackerie calls,' Gail said. 'I wish it smelt like this.' She leant over the gate and inhaled strenuously. 'Which do you like best? The scent of roses or this new-mown grass?'

'It's one of Mr Hustler's days to do the garden.' Magdalen chose not to answer the question. The fragrance rising from the lawns and the great blooms nauseated her.

'My sense of smell stopped functioning in childhood,' she murmured to herself as she took a path through shrubberies to the back of the house. 'No, it didn't stop functioning; it was distorted, twisted, screwed up.'

Two

On the kitchen table there was a note propped against a plant. Both the note and the plant had been left by Mrs Brook who came to clean and manage the house. 'I dropped in to wish you luck, I'm sorry I missed you,' she had written. 'I've left Eddie Rutter repairing the hall light. Please don't water this hibiscus, I've seen to it. Keeping my fingers crossed! C. Brook.'

In the hall, Eddie Rutter was standing on a plank that bridged two ladders. Wires drooped from the ceiling. He greeted her with: 'Hi, there! A pity you weren't home half an hour since. I could've done with another pair of hands.'

'I was going to look at it myself. I enjoy jobs like that.'

'I wish I did. Clara Brook told me it's the great day. How did you do? Or shouldn't I ask?'

'I did all right.' She smiled back at him, at last able to acknowledge her success. Any moment, she thought, I'll make an exhibition of myself, give myself a hernia laughing, yell: I've done it!

'I'm hungry,' she said.

'The electricity for the cooker and such isn't off. They're on a different circuit.'

'I know.'

11

'Doing yourself a toasted sandwich to celebrate?'

'Something like that.'

He doesn't know what I have to celebrate, Magdalen thought as she strode back to the kitchen. He thinks it's for getting good grades. Everyone else will, too: the right grades and into university – what I set my mind on. And they're right, but that's not the half of it. I'll say I've something to celebrate! And it's a lot more than they think.

She grabbed the telephone on the dresser and dialled rapidly. 'I'd like a re-style, wash and dry. Could you fit me in? Like in half an hour? Who? Oh, Magdalen Wilde.' She tapped the handset impatiently while the appointments book was consulted, then: 'Thanks. That's fine. I have to be back at work for half-one. No, I'm not going anywhere. I just feel like a new look.'

That makes a start, she congratulated herself. It's not exactly revolutionary but it's early days yet. 'You'll be looking forward to Edinburgh, starting a new life,' Mr Gresham said. Right again, but he doesn't know it all. In fact, he hasn't the first idea. You have to know what the old life's been like before you can say a new one is starting.

She sawed at a loaf, the knife jerking as she laughed. I've hit my target: escape. No compromise, no weakening. Final, total escape. She spooned peanut butter on to the bread. She was ravenous. All she had eaten that day was a few dusty crisps.

Since then, her hopes had been realised. Freedom was guaranteed. Soon she would leave this house. Leave *him*.

Years before, when she had run away, she had always

been caught and brought back. She was too young and ignorant to win against him, Lindsay Wilde with his easy contacts, position and power. He could pay people to find her. So, despairing, she had given up.

She was no more optimistic several years later, though by then she could have left home; like Paul Driffield. Because, he said, his parents were Nazis. Compared with hers, with her father, Paul's were a couple of saints. As far as I know, Magdalen added, sombre. However, she had not followed Paul's example. Hopeless, she had thought: There's no point. Having my own place won't keep Dad out of it. He'll come after me, give me no peace. I'd never be free of him that way.

Then, this year, he had been obliged to work abroad and for eight glorious months she had been beyond his control. She had led her own life; he had been unable to take charge. This was the stuff of dreams. She felt as if for years she had been clamped in a vice, but suddenly it had loosened. She was allowed to stretch; the oxygen could course through her blood, flexing the muscles and brain.

Invigorated, she had looked at herself and said, 'This is *me*. I'm not waggling at the end of his string. This is what it's like to be by myself.'

And she had thought: Why can't it be like this always? Why must it stop when he returns home? Until one day she had told herself: This doesn't have to stop when he comes back. It can go on. I shan't let him take me over. Never again. I shan't let him rule me. Bold with the possibility of permanent freedom, she declared: 'I don't care when he comes back. It doesn't matter because I shall clear out.'

As she said this, she felt the final twist of the vice give way. Released at last, she danced round the house, stood in every room and passage, and shouted, 'I shan't be here!'

The way to achieve this was to go to university. It was foolproof. People would not see it as running away but as a legitimate reason to leave home and her father would accept it. He had always wished her to excel and it would not occur to him that he could lose her; he would plan to visit her, organise expensive holidays and look forward to the long vacations when she was at home. What he would not suspect was that she held a trump card: she would be living in a Hall of Residence or a Student House.

In either of these Magdalen calculated she would be safe. When he came to see her she would not be alone, there would be plenty of people about and she could make sure that he never entered her room. On the campus and in a Hall or University lodging, Magdalen considered that she would be protected. Invulnerable.

The kind of accommodation she needed was reserved, provided that she applied for it by the first of next month and, deciding to look in the prospectus to check procedure, Magdalen left the kitchen. As she walked through the hall, the telephone rang.

'If that's Roy,' Eddie Rutter said, 'd'you mind telling him I've about done?' Poised with a screwdriver, he waited until she had lifted the handset and mouthed: Not for you.

The voice that greeted her was strong, resonant with

loving. 'Oh, Magdalen! What wonderful news! You've done splendidly.'

'Thanks.' She wished she could have avoided giving him this satisfaction. 'How do you know?'

'I called Harley Gresham before lunch. I imagine you've been trying to get through. Unfortunately, these lines have been busy all morning.'

'I haven't had a minute.'

'I'm sure. Harley tells me that all his candidates have done well this year but your results were outstanding. We talked for some time.'

I bet. 'I'll be in at Edinburgh.'

'Yes. That was something else we discussed and, thinking it over, I've decided to come home. It will give us a chance to celebrate as well.'

'When?' The handset was shaking.

'When should we celebrate? Tomorrow. I've asked Jean to book a table at The King's.'

'I meant, when will you be arriving?'

'Not until the last flight this evening, I'm afraid. I have to ensure that Andrew's fully briefed.'

She could see that Eddie was watching her. With a great effort she steadied her hand and smiled into the mouthpiece. 'Do you want me to get you a meal?'

'I'd love that, but I'd better say no. There'll be food of sorts on the plane and it won't do any harm to starve a little before our celebratory feast. I look forward to being with you. And, precious, how is my rose?'

'Much the same as usual.'

'I've missed it.'

15

Duly she continued this code between them. 'Aren't there any in Holland?'

'Not the sort I like.'

As she put down the handset, Eddie asked, 'Who's your boy-friend, then, Mag?'

Three

Returning home from the petrol station in the late afternoon, Magdalen went through the back gates and pushed her cycle into the garage. Her father's car had been washed and the bodywork meticulously waxed. So Mr Hustler had received a message that her father was coming home. The car gleamed, smug, immaculate, soon to be claimed by its owner. Agitated, Magdalen hunched her shoulders like someone who hoped to avoid detection, crept between greenhouses and round a neat pond. Reaching the house door, she opened it carefully, knowing the exact angle before it would creak. In the hall she tiptoed from rug to muffling rug so that her heels would not tap on the stone. When she heard footsteps outside, she leapt for the stairs. But the only sound that followed was the rattle of the letter-box and the thud of a newspaper on the mat.

As she waited for her breathing to quieten, Magdalen thought: Talk about being conditioned! I only need to see his car ready for him and I take fright. Even though he's been home only three week-ends this year, a total of one hundred and eight hours. He won't stay more than a couple of nights. And in less than two months, I shall have gone.

She climbed up to the room which had progressed from

her toy store to her work place. From the window-seat she could see Mr Hustler straightening the edges of a lawn. He was staying late to prepare the garden ready for inspection. That was unnecessary; it always was. She watched him chop his spade into the grass and slice away slim turves. He had been there as long as she could remember. 'Come and smell,' he had invited and lifted her up until her face was close to a bloom but, wanting Panda to smell it, she had pushed his snout into the petals. 'Now you stop that!' Mr Hustler had reprimanded. 'I don't want that rose damaging.' But she had slapped at it, made it swing on its stalk before he had lowered her on to the grass. 'If I were your father,' he had threatened. Frightened, she had run away, across the lawn, through the kitchen, along the passage, up two flights of stairs and into the attic.

Magdalen found she was leaning into the curtain, gripping the fabric in a tight fist. He won't be home before twenty-one twenty, she soothed herself.

In the garden Mr Hustler had reached a path exactly where her father used to stand. He used to look up, see her at the window and wave. Hang on to that, she urged herself. Think of the good times. He would wave. Then he'd do his hat trick.

Despite the frowns of Mr Hustler, her father would toss his hat into the air and catch it on his head, wave to her again, and throw a leg over an imaginary horse. Then he would flick the reins and canter to the back gate. He had given her a tricycle for Christmas, the favourite of all her toys. Mr Hustler didn't approve of it. He would follow the marks of the tyres to where she was hidden behind the greenhouse and snarl, his teeth nicotine brown, 'You stay off the lawns. I can't keep them decent if you take that thing over them. I'll tell your father if you don't do as I say.'

Fifteen years later Magdalen looked at Mr Hustler drive his spade into the soil and creak upright. An old, tired man.

And fifteen years later she had determined to write it all down. She had wanted to get it straight before she moved on. She had said, 'Move on', keeping her fingers crossed that her plan would succeed and increasing her studying hours. If I can describe it, she had thought, it will be finished with; I can leave it behind me. Yet she had not begun.

'It's all such a jumble,' she murmured. 'It flies in every direction or just comes back to me in bits. I'm not sure when a lot of the bits happened. They flip out of sequence. I don't like that; it prevents me from getting things clear. I'd rather have everything in the right order.' But these were not science A levels. They were memories.

'I'm making excuses for not starting,' she admitted. 'I promised myself I'd begin as soon as the examinations were over, then after I'd had a rest, then when I'd got the results. But now Dad's coming.'

She paused, her eyes on the creases she had made in the curtain. At last she said, 'If I postpone getting down to it because he'll be here tonight, I'll never have the guts to do anything else.'

Magdalen left the window-seat, crossed to the table, switched on her word processor, put the start disk through and inserted one already formatted. Creating a document, she wrote in a title: Autobiography. Then she regarded the word. Her life, so far. She had kept it all in her head for so long that she had feared her hold would slip and something would snap. But nothing's snapped, I'm sane, she tapped out. Though Dad once said that I could be locked up. One of his nastier threats.

She wiped the screen then it stared at her, its emptiness accusing; her fingers would not move again across the keyboard and she was very hot. The great wedge of window was never turned away from the sun but that did not explain why her lungs would soon stop working, why her throat was closing up. She risked that whenever she allowed the memories to come back. She must find a way of overcoming these sensations. Work out a strategy.

She looked round the room. Gail had called it a turret and, her thoughts wandering to Melanie Howkins' cousin – what was he called? Greg – she remembered Gail telling her: 'He's off to Armley Gaol . . . it's built like a castle . . . doing a series of illustrations . . . some kind of fairy-tale . . . only he wants it to be modern.'

Magdalen realised that her throat had relaxed again and her breath, unhindered, whispered: A turret. A tower. A castle. A prisoner. A princess. That was the solution. And her fingers were on the keyboard, entering:

FROM PRINCESS TO PRISONER
(containing an appendix, *Plans and Preparations for Escape*.)

'Once upon a time . . .'

Magdalen ran the eraser through the phrase and began again. 'Long ago there was a little girl who lived in a turret in a big house.' This, too, was wiped. After several more jabs at a first sentence, Magdalen tried, 'Long ago there was a castle,' changed it to: 'We will begin with the castle,' and continued to write.

It stands by itself on the top of a high mountain and can be seen many miles away. It is not especially big and since it has roses leaning against its walls and the window in its tower twinkles in the sun, it has quite a domestic appearance. So when visitors approach the castle, their eyes are blind to the moat that surrounds it and their ears are deaf to the echo of their steps upon the great drawbridge. When they ring the bell at the huge gates they do not notice the portcullis poised above their heads and they do not catch sight of the men-at-arms guarding the battlements. They are not aware that this castle, like all of its kind, is a fortress. It was built to repel invaders, intruders and curious people.

The walls of this castle are built of heavy stone too thick for sounds to penetrate and from its large ceremonial hall stretch windowless passages lined with closed doors. One of these is covered with green baize and secured with two iron bolts. Behind are steps which lead down to the dungeon. This is not the only place where it is wise not to venture, for above, among the bed chambers, there are dark niches, cupboards and closets that are airless and without natural light. Here is to be found, cunningly hidden under fine linen and silken robes, the family skeleton, and in the night-time out of a closet sneaks the castle's ghost.

In the beginning, three people lived in this castle: a father, a mother and their child. The father called the child My Princess, so she knew this meant he was king and her mother was queen. The king had other names for his princess, like Precious and Special, and one day as together they played in the garden he gave a new name to one of his roses, calling it Precious Princess.

Because the king's realm stretched far beyond the castle walls, every morning he lifted the door of the stable and backed out his great snorting charger who was named Merk. With a wave to the queen and the princess, he would gallop away. Then the lady-in-waiting would brush the queen's hair and together they would bath the princess and rub her dry until her cheeks shone. The chambermaids would sweep out the castle and the cook would prepare an elegant meal for the king's return. That was always exciting because the king brought toys for the princess and flowers for the queen. He never gave her roses from the gardens which surrounded the castle. Those he guarded as fiercely as golden treasure and only the gardener was permitted to touch.

This gardener had a red face, his head was bald and the digging had given him a stoop. Perhaps that is why he was bad-tempered. He was a loyal servant and he worked diligently in the garden, weeding between the flowers and pruning the shrubs. But the task he most liked was attending to the lawns. He mowed and raked and rolled the dense grass until it was smooth and shining as velvet.

Every day the gardener rode to the castle on a squeaking and mud-splattered mule and when he had hitched it to the fence he would walk round the castle walls until he came to a flight of steps. These were hidden behind a trellis on which he had trained roses, but the princess had seen the steps and she knew that at the bottom of them was a big black door. One day she asked the gardener, 'What is there?' 'Never you mind,' he answered. Bravely she followed him. 'But what's in there?' she asked again, pointing to the door. The gardener took out a big key and replied, 'Something. Don't you be nosey.' 'Tell me what it is,' she persisted. The gardener glared at her and tutted impatiently. 'It's a monster I keep for chasing after naughty children and I'll let it out this minute if you don't buzz off.' Then he put the key in the lock, but before he turned it, the princess turned away.

The princess did not tell the king what the gardener had said to her. If she had, the king might have asked her if she had been naughty and she wasn't sure what she should answer. So she sat quietly on the rug in front of the hearth where logs sent corkscrew flames up the chimney and she coloured in her book, pleased if the king suggested what crayons she should choose. If the queen, who some-times lay on the sofa, asked for a glass of water, the princess would pour it out. When the king told her that she must go to bed, the princess did not argue because she always tried to obey his commands. However, he made them easier. He scrubbed her teeth and gave her a piggyback to her bedroom and helped her to undress. Then he arranged her duvet over her and kissed her good-night.

Thus the princess was happy. She was loved by the king and his queen and she liked living in the castle. It was warm and safe. She did not know then that the castle was a fortress, and that soon it would have secrets to guard.

The only blemish on her happiness was the gardener. He remained, always digging and tending the roses and watching. Watching to see if she made a mistake.

There were noises somewhere in the house. Gradually shedding the pictures in her mind, Magdalen concentrated on the sound, a continuous double beat. She pressed the key for save and, descending the attic stairs, ignored the telephone ringing in her father's room and went down to the one in the hall.

'Is there anything wrong with your phone?' Gail asked.

'I don't know. Is there?'

'You sound far away. Look, Mag, do you want any . . .'

There was a draught in the hall; it found her bare neck. The hairdresser had said, 'I don't like to do this, Magdalen. Have you thought of how your father's going to take it? He likes it shoulder length.'

She had answered, 'One inch from the scalp, please, and not a millimetre more.'

'I'm reinventing myself,' she told Gail. 'I've had my hair–'

'You haven't answered my question.'

'Sorry. Come again?'

'Do you want any help tomorrow?'

'Help?'

'Will you concentrate? Watch my lips. Would-you-like-me-to-come-to-mor-row-some-time-to-help-you-get-read-y-for-the-par-ty?'

Tomorrow. A party. She had blocked it off immediately she had heard that he was arriving. 'Gail. Crisis. My dad's telephoned. He's flying back home this evening. Because of the results. He'll be at Leeds-Bradford at twenty-one hours. Is my watch right? Is it really twenty-fifty?'

'Quarter-to. Oh, Mag, isn't that marvellous of him!'

'I have to get ready.' He would expect her to be wearing her 'special togs'. For a moment Magdalen stiffened, then reminded herself: Not many more times.

'Yes, you go and smarten up. What about the party?'

'Damn.' The party belonged to another world. 'It's no good. It can't be here. I don't know exactly when Dad'll be going back. Sunday, I expect, or early next week.'

'Shall I phone round?'

'Thanks, Gail. You've saved my life. Say I'll get in touch.'

In the bathroom Magdalen stripped and looked at herself in the mirror. After the examinations she had spent a lot of time at the town's outdoor pool gaining a tan but this evening it gave her no satisfaction. It followed the line of her bikini and, in contrast, her skin looked whiter, her breasts more prominent. 'Like they're drawing attention,' she said to herself.

Disgusted, she turned from her reflection but before stepping into the shower she opened the bathroom cabinet. Behind her toothpaste, the shampoo, make-up and sleeping tablets, she had hidden, well out of her sight, the toilet items which belonged to her father. Hurriedly she brought them to the front: gels, after-shave lotion, skin freshener, deodorant. Every fragrance.

So Magdalen prepared for her father's return.

Four

Although she had gone to bed late, Magdalen was up early the next morning. She was determined to continue her fairy story before leaving for work. 'He shan't prevent me,' she told herself and repeated the words like a charm to exorcise his presence. Downstairs in the kitchen she poured out a dish of cereals and ate them quickly before making a beaker of tea. Fishing out the bag, she asked, 'Shall I take him a cup?' Last night he had looked tired; happy to be home and to be with her, but so tired. Soon he'll be old, she thought, needing her in a different way; she felt pity for him and an unexpected, irrational remorse. 'My precious!' he had greeted her, dropping his case, his arms wide stretched, and it was impossible for her to evade the embrace. Can't he see? Doesn't he suspect? she had thought, his lips on her throat. 'You're looking wonderful,' he had told her. 'Success suits you.' You bet, she said to herself as she picked up her beaker of tea and turned her back on the caddy containing his special blend beside the handsome bone-china pot. He had said, 'You've had your hair cut,' and later, a hand cupping his brandy glass: 'I'm afraid I don't like it as short, but you can let it grow.' He had smiled, complacent, sure that she would.

27

Magdalen climbed to her attic work place, her tower, and sat at the word processor. She ran through to the end of the document and read out: 'He remained digging and tending the roses and watching. Watching to see if she made a mistake.' She looked at her fingers, instructed them to loosen, and began a new paragraph.

It has been said that in the castle lived three people only, the king, his queen and his princess, but there came another.

One night, after she had kissed the king and queen goodnight, the princess curled up under her duvet and went to sleep. She did not know how long she had been there when suddenly she was awake. It was dark and the castle was quiet but there was a noise close at hand. Feet were pacing slowly backwards and forwards outside her door. She made a small squeaking cry but it was not loud enough to be heard through the thick walls. She dared not jump out of her bed and run into the next chamber where the king and queen slept. Before she reached them, she knew she would be caught. So she remained, her eyes open, and listened until the sounds went away.

The following morning while the king prepared himself to visit his kingdom, the princess went to the queen. 'Last night someone was walking outside my door,' she told her and the queen answered, 'It must have been a dream. No one has entered this castle. The locks are still fastened, the bolts are firm in the casing and the drawbridge is up. Do not be afraid.

There can be neither intruder nor trespasser.' Therefore the princess agreed that she had dreamt of the footsteps and for many nights afterwards she went to bed without apprehension, believing the castle was safe.

But sometime later the princess heard the noise again, and again she attempted to summon the king and queen and again she was too afraid. 'I heard the person last night,' she told the king while he was having breakfast, and she began to cry. 'What an imagination you have, precious! Our castle is secure. The locks are still fastened, the bolts are shot and the drawbridge is raised. No person could penetrate these thick walls. Only a ghost could do that, and a ghost cannot harm you. However, this evening I will bring you something that will shield you and keep you from harm.' Knowing that she could trust the king's word, the princess dried her tears and she waited to receive this special protection. At the end of the day the king returned to the castle bearing a large parcel. Inside was a duvet cover printed all over with pictures of Paddington Bear. The queen tutted, saying that they possessed plenty of covers already but the king shook his head and smiled at the princess in a way that said: We know that this is no ordinary cover, don't we? The princess folded her arms across it, pleased with their secret, and smiled back. Then together the king and the princess raced up the stairs, shook her duvet out of its bag and pushed it into this new one. They poked and jabbed and slapped until it was completely inside. Paddington Bear, so thin and flat before, grew fat and important. 'See,' the king said. 'He is your knight in armour. He will defend you and permit no ghost to touch.' This made the princess glad, for nothing could reach her. The king was king. He was her favourite. He knew how to stop ghosts. Paddington Bear on her duvet cover proved that.

Thus, once more for a time the princess was satisfied. Each evening, after she had kissed the queen, the king would carry her to bed and pull the duvet up to her chin. Over the mound he would kiss her good-night. After he had left her she would push her fingers into her ears, not because she doubted Paddington Bear's vigilance but because she preferred not to hear the sound of the ghost. But gradually her anxiety returned and alone in her turret, playing with her toys, she tried to work it out. She was a curious child and given to questions. And the question was: Do ghosts make a noise? She was certain that was not their custom. Pictures showed them like wraiths, boneless and without feet. So this castle ghost was different. It could do something that no other ghost could do. This frightened her. She went to the king and told him and he replied, 'Unhappy ghosts make noises. Let us hope that one day this ghost will be happy again.'

Although she could not help being afraid of the ghost, the suggestion that it might be unhappy worried the princess. The thought of it entered her sleep, shivering her body with its chill. Waking, she found Paddington Bear over her shoulders, alert and standing sentry, so she knew that he had kept her safe. When she told the king, he said, 'Of course he did. You can rely on that bear,' and he laughed. Nevertheless he seemed sad; his face was pale and there were black crescents under his eyes.

Magdalen heard the curtains drawn back in the room below her then the door of a wardrobe open. She did not wish to meet her father but luckily it was time for her to leave. Working at the petrol station was an undeniable excuse to avoid him. It was odd, having to bother with that after these last months. She pressed the key for save, withdrew the disk and put it in her bag. As far as she knew, her father didn't pry into her belongings, but she wasn't taking the risk. Just another little secret, she mouthed to him through the floor. I can keep them as well as you. I've had years of practice. She added a notebook to the litter in her bag, thinking she might have the opportunity to continue the story while at work. As she passed her father's bedroom, he called, 'Good morning, precious. Do come in.'

'Can't. Haven't time. I'm off.'

'Surely not! I can't spare more than a couple of days.'

Any moment he would be opening the door, confronting her with his disappointment. She went down the stairs in three leaps and shouted up from the hall, 'It's too late to call off. I don't want to lose my job,' and muttered, 'In other words, I want the wage.' When she left home she was determined to have her own money, not his.

Running down the path towards the garages, she came upon Mr Hustler. 'Fine day,' he greeted.

'Yes,' she said, for the first time noticing.

'I hope your father got home without trouble.'

'Yes, thanks.'

'I wanted a word.'

'He's getting up.'

The man walked with her, obliging her to slacken her pace, muttering to himself, 'Must have left that ball of twine in my saddle-bag.'

As he watched Magdalen wheel out her bicycle, he told her, 'That machine's growing rust.'

'It's the fertiliser I put on it.'

'Still, if it goes.'

'It'll break the sound barrier with a following wind.'

'You want to be careful, traffic like it is.'

'I'll be late, Mr Hustler.' She had never used a less formal address.

'You don't change much.'

'I'm having a go.'

'I remember. You gave me some moil. A terror you were, on that trike.'

She laughed, his remark was so banal. That was his memory. He stood in the doorway of the garage, a pair of secateurs in a hand, gazing at the lawns he lovingly tended; and she stared at him, bridging the years.

There were tyre marks in the grass where the wheels of the tricycle had slid off the path. No, they had not slid; they had been steered. Looking behind her, she shook at the sight of what she had done and she ran back along the narrow grooves stamping, trying to erase them but they wouldn't disappear and she dropped down on her stomach and crawled under a bush. Then Mr Hustler's hands were on her legs, they pushed up to her knees then further still and fastened, and she was dragged out. Immediately Mr Hustler's face was right up to hers and his mouth was growling,' If you were my girl I'd put you across my knee, drop your bloomers and take a slipper to your bottom till you couldn't sit down.'

'Yes, I was pleased to see the back of that trike,' Mr Hustler added, reminiscent, and was astonished as without farewell Magdalen jumped on her bicycle and shot out of the garage. 'She's always been a funny lass,' he explained to his secateurs, 'and she wants to mind out. That road isn't what it was; gets traffic.'

While pedalling hectically, Magdalen wrote in her head:

He had magic. 'Just look at the roses!' the king would exclaim. 'The fellow's a wizard.' The princess knew wizards had magic, so that was how the gardener did what he did. He let out the Monster he kept for chasing naughty children and he sent it into the castle. But it was a little time before the princess understood.

The first night it came, trespassing into her dreams, it made a draught on her pillow which stayed there until she was roused. Then it drew away. With her eyes open, the presence that had visited her sleep

33

still in the room, she called for the king and queen but only a whisper crept from her mouth. The place by her bed became empty again and the quiet seeped back. The princess pulled her duvet over her head and listened to the drumming of her heart. For she had discovered that Paddington Bear could protect her only against ghosts; those were the instructions the king had given him. Her knight in armour was powerless against anything else. The unhappy ghost had been replaced by a creature that took no account of Paddington Bear.

It was the next night, when she smelt the odour of roses and the new-mown grass, that the princess knew what this creature was and who had sent it. The gardener had walked down the steps behind the trellis of roses and with his big key he had unlocked the black door. Then he had opened a door in the passage that stretched from the kitchen into the castle hall. That was the door covered in green baize and secured by two iron bolts. The queen had said, 'The bolts are firm in their casing and the drawbridge is up; there can be neither intruder nor trespasser.' She had forgotten the gardener was a wizard. He had used his magic to penetrate the door and shoot back the bolts. Then he had ordered his monster to find the princess.

And when it had gone, had at last taken away its cold and dibbling fingers, the princess lay with her knees bent into her chest and her nightgown held tight over her feet, and she said to herself: This is for being naughty; it is for riding my tricycle over the lawns and for showing my legs to the gardener. Because, if she was being punished, it meant she had been bad. That is what she had been taught.

She did not tell anyone. She did not tell Joanna, the lady-in-waiting, that the gardener-wizard had used his magic and sent a monster to punish her. Joanna would have laughed and said, 'You're a one, always dreaming. Come here, let me give you a cuddle. There aren't any real monsters; they are only in fairy-tales.' She did not tell the queen because the doctor who visited the castle had patted her head and whispered, 'Try not to bother your mother too much.' Nor did she tell the king because he would have asked her what she had done to deserve this punishment and then he, too, would have been cross.

I don't know how I can keep this up, Magdalen said to herself as she reached the petrol station. Every time I think about it, I feel that I'm about to pass out. And this is only the beginning.

'You shouldn't push that bike so hard,' a mechanic observed. 'You'll bust a tyre. Or a lung.'

'Could be.' However, later, she was calm enough to return to the paragraphs she had composed and she managed to scribble them down. She even added:

For a few days after the monster had visited her, the princess stayed in the attic playing with her toys, but she longed for her tricycle. So eventually she returned to the garden and rode along the paths. She did her best not to let the tricycle turn on to the lawn and the monster was pleased with her for trying to be good. Though he did not speak, he told her by making his hands warmer and by the way he stroked.

After that, Magdalen put the notebook away. The place was too public for such a story. Could be habit forming, she cautioned herself; I'll be putting it out on loudspeakers and offering it to the sob slot on Radio One.

Through the window she saw a customer pull into the forecourt. He reversed and advanced until he judged his petrol tank was likely to be within range of a pump, then he turned his attention to the next problem which was to open the car door. After a thorough search of the interior, he eventually succeeded, examined the petrol dispenser, wrenched a pipe from its moorings and pushed it into the tank. The figure on the display panel recording the sale raced, stopped, recommenced and stopped again as he tried to reach exactly five pounds. Then there was a clang and he was holding the nozzle at arm's length and stamping petrol off his boots. Still game, he approached the car bonnet, ran a finger along the edge, pressed, tried to lever it up with a thumb-nail, knelt and angled his head under the bumper. Finding no clue, he walked across to the office and asked her, 'Do you have any idea how to open that bonnet?'

'Why don't you know how to open it? Is the car nicked?'

'That's right. It's breaking into the bonnet that separates the men from the boys. I know you. You're Magdalen something. I didn't recognise you with your hair off.'

'I didn't recognise you with your hair on.'

'I'm Greg Howkins. I was up at the school yesterday.'

'It's coming back. Gail talked to you.'

'Gail?'

'She looks like a biker but she isn't. She rents her brother's leathers. Says it gives her confidence.'

'They seem to work.'

'You car's blocking the pump. I'll open the bonnet.'

'Melanie asked me to check the oil,' he explained as he followed Magdalen to the car.

She pulled the lever that was under the steering column and the bonnet sprang open. Then she located the catch, heaved the bonnet up and fixed it on the supporting rod.

'I'm impressed,' Greg said. 'You wouldn't happen to be able to identify the dip stick, would you?'

'Do you know anything at all about cars?'

'Not a lot.'

As she went through the routine of examining the oil level he said, 'I don't think I'll try for a job in a petrol station.'

'It's a useful place to be if you want to thumb a lift. Now what does this say to you?' She showed him the bars on the dip stick.

'It says, "I'm full." '

'Correct.'

'You're as good with the dip stick as you are at passing exams.'

'It's not easy to get decent grades.'

'I know. Otherwise I might have done.'

'I thought you were mocking.'

'Why should I do that?'

She shrugged but when she was back behind the till and he was paying for the petrol, she said, 'I had to get into a medical school.'

'Melanie told me.'

'Miss Howkins is OK. Different.'

He was her cousin. But also from outside, someone who didn't make assumptions. And suddenly she confided, 'I do sincerely want to read medicine but what I most want is to get away.'

He would have said: So what's new? but something in her expression, sombre and intense, stopped him and he merely nodded.

'I don't mean only from home.' She halted, seemed to gather herself to say more but the words caught in her throat and she was leaning on the counter, coughing, her face crimson as she retched.

'Steady!' Greg stretched across and thumped her between the shoulder blades. When she was quieter he opened a bottle of lemonade from the shelf and told her to take a drink.

'Thanks. You'd make a good nurse.'

'I already have. Well, that's one name for it.'

'What are the others?'

'Cleaner, shopper, barber, mopper-upper. I've done things like being a home help, worked in a day centre. There's more, too, but . . .' He made a gesture towards the telephone that had begun to ring. 'I'll go. See you later. Eight, isn't it?'

'What?' she demanded as she lifted the handset but he had gone and Gail's voice was coming along the line.

'Mag? That you? I've only got a second — there's a coach party of wrinklies, all of them ordering toasted scones. I just thought I'd better let you know it's sorted.'

'Know what's sorted?' If she thought hard, she'd work out what Greg meant.

'I can't believe it! There I've been, worried I might miss someone, and when they weren't in, up at the crack of dawn, calling them out of bed grumbling, and my mother asking why doesn't Magdalen do her own phoning and don't I have a conscience about the bill and when I tell you, all you can say . . . Hell! Isn't your father the most dishy? He's across the road. I can see him from where I'm standing at the phone.'

'Gail, *please*. I'm sorry I didn't get you straight away. I was thinking about something else.' She knew now why Greg had said, 'See you later.'

'It doesn't matter. I'm not surprised your mind's not on it. He's come out of Lavinia's Lingerie and he's carrying a parcel.'

Magdalen closed her eyes. This evening he would say, 'I've a present for you, the latest frivolity.' The last two or three had been negligées, diaphanous, threaded with ribbon and lace.

Gail was asking, 'Do you suppose he's bought something for a woman he's got? Do you think he might marry again?'

'That'd be the day.'

'He looks really good. Better, I'd say, if that's possible.'

'Oh, come on, Gail. What're you sickening for? Gerontophilia?'

'I happen to know what that means, and I might if all chaps his age were like him.'

'Can you stop drooling and pay attention? Greg Howkins doesn't know the party's off.'

'I asked Matthew to give him a message.'

'Well, he hasn't got it. He was in a few minutes ago for petrol and when you came on the phone, he went, murmuring he'd be seeing me soon. "Eight, isn't it?" he said. I didn't understand him.'

'For someone who's so good at organising herself, you're the pits. You'll have to phone Miss Howkins, and I'll try as well.'

Despite frequent attempts during the rest of the day, Magdalen failed to get through. Either there was no answer or the line was engaged. 'Perhaps when there's somebody already on, it's Gail,' she said to herself, 'but that could be a long chance. What did Dad say about going out to dinner this evening? Table booked for twenty hours and leaving home at nineteen forty. That's lucky. If Greg does turn up, Dad and I will have gone.

Five

Magdalen had not imagined that Greg might arrive early.

Her shift at the petrol station did not finish until seven but she was in no hurry to leave. Telling herself she was not obliged to rush in order to comply with her father's meticulous planning, she loitered, chatted to the evening attendant, then took the longest way home. About to enter the house, she heard the crack of gravel under wheels, so she turned back and walked on to the drive. A small red hatchback was approaching and through the windscreen she could see the faces of Melanie Howkins and Greg. Alarmed, Magdalen flagged them down, mouthed at the passenger window, 'The party's off,' and waved her arms to suggest that Melanie reverse. Interpreting these gestures to indicate there was an obstruction ahead, Melanie craned forward to see round the bend while Greg struggled with his window. Before he had succeeded in lowering it, Magdalen caught sight of her father descending the front steps. Immediately she left them and walked towards him.

'Visitors?' he asked, then looking at his watch, 'I'd hoped you'd be home before now.'

'I was held up at the garage,' she told him without a

41

blink. 'I don't think you've met Miss Howkins, Dad,' and she led him to the car.

Introduced, he said to Melanie, 'I must have missed you at the various school functions. To my regret.'

'I haven't taught there very long. This is Greg, my cousin.'

The two men nodded, murmured acknowledgements.

To suggest that she, too, was being introduced, Magdalen said, 'Hi, you look as if you're making for a party.' There was a pack of cans on his lap.

For a moment he hesitated then answered, 'That's right.'

Melanie added quickly, 'I'm about to drop him off.'

Lindsay Wilde was not deceived by their attempts to appear natural but he gave no hint in his manner. He said to Melanie, 'I'm interested in this car you're driving. How do you find it?'

'Fine, although it's a bit sluggish in cold weather for the first couple of miles.'

'That's exactly what I've been told. For which reason I'm thinking of the 1.6. For Magdalen when she's passed the test.'

'That seems a pretty substantial inducement.'

Lindsay Wilde frowned. 'I regard driving as an essential skill nowadays and most young people are eager to acquire it.'

Glancing at his daughter, Melanie detected a stubbornness round her mouth, the muscles flexing in her cheeks, and she thought: Is it the licence or the car she's objecting to? To Lindsay Wilde she remarked, 'A lot of

Magdalen's generation consider that bicycles are more environmentally sound.'

The man laughed briefly and made a gesture, dismissive. The hand had been recently manicured; rather too beautifully, Melanie thought. For no intelligible reason she shuddered.

Then Greg asked Magdalen, 'Are you going?'

He was daring her to stop the pretence. 'To the party? I haven't been invited.'

'No hassle. I can bring anyone I wish.'

She laughed. 'That sounds risky. Sounds like the sort of party that gets called off. Anyway, I've got a date.'

Behind her, her father was explaining, 'I'm treating Magdalen to a celebratory dinner.'

'She has a lot to celebrate,' Melanie Howkins said.

'And may I thank you for your part in it?'

'I don't claim much. Magdalen did the work. And she could motivate herself. I didn't have to offer inducements.'

Lindsay Wilde nodded and he and Melanie stared at each other, surprised at the strength of their mutual dislike.

As she put the car into reverse, Melanie said, 'I'm not desperate for the book, Magdalen. It was just that I thought I could pick it up as I was passing.' Thus she invented a reason for their visit. 'You can drop it in any time.'

'Thank you.'

'What an extraordinary young man!' Lindsay Wilde exclaimed as they walked into the house.

'Why do you say that?'

By now he knew that Magdalen had made an arrangement for this evening that had been cancelled because of his return and he did not wish to be bothered with details. But he could not ignore Greg. 'He hadn't known you three minutes before he was inviting you to accompany him to a party.'

She asked herself: Why didn't I accept the invitation? Why didn't I leap into the back seat? Tell Greg: You're on. Say to Dad: Sorry, you'll have to cancel the table; you didn't *ask* me whether I wanted to have dinner with you; now I have an *invitation* and I'm accepting that. What would have happened? Would her father have dragged her out of the car? Given plausible arguments to shame her into compliance?

No. He would have done neither. He would have been unruffled, indulgent, gracious, fetching her a bottle to take with her. Concealing his anger. Before the other two her father would have kept the public mask unspotted and without a crack. As he had for years. As she had, too, trained to obedience.

'Personally I found his approach rather crude,' her father was saying. His arm circled her shoulders. 'Perhaps I'm a little out of date.'

Magdalen went up the stairs. From the bathroom came the scents of her father's shower gel and body lotions. On the table by her bed, standing in a slender vase of crystal, was a single crimson rose: the Precious Princess.

In this way did her father prepare for the dinner and its sequel.

* * *

The rose had gone the next morning and in its place was a tray bearing her breakfast. Still drowsy, after a sleep that had not refreshed her, Magdalen watched a gauze of cream form on top of the coffee, the slice of fried bacon stiffen and the yolk of the egg congeal. He had brought it up as he always did after such an occasion, fussing, apologising for the apron over his pyjamas, for his unshaven chin, but declaring that her breakfast was more important, telling her how much he had enjoyed the evening; she had given him new life. What it was to be seen with such a marvellous young woman on his arm!

The breakfast brought to her bed was her customary reward, and it meant that she had not said it to him last night. The words had been planned but had not been uttered. She had not insisted in a shout that penetrated the walls: 'No! No! Let me alone. I don't belong to you. I belong to myself. From now on, it is not you calling the tune; it's me. I'm doing what *I* want to do.'

Why had the words lodged in her throat? Why hadn't she cried out against him? She had done that when she was younger. Once, when she was a child.

The gardener continued to send the monster and although the princess was frightened, she did not cry out. If she had, she was certain that the punishment would become more severe. She believed that the monster would eat her up. This idea terrified her when, after its fingers, there came its lips.

But one night she did not keep silent because the

monster made a mistake. It was the first time it spoke to her. It called her 'my special' just as the king did and it spoke in the king's voice. This caused the princess much consternation and she asked silently, 'Can this be the king?' Then she answered, 'No, it cannot be the king my father because he is asleep with the queen and he loves me; he would not do this.' And she was sorry that she had asked, 'Is this the king?' even in her thoughts. She told herself firmly, 'It is the magic that borrows the king's voice for the monster to use.' This frightened the princess even more than ever. For if the magic could give the king's voice to the monster, it might change all of him into the king, and then how would she be able to distinguish which one was which? So, although her throat was so parched she could hardly say it, she whispered, 'I'll tell.' 'What shall you tell?' the monster asked her, its mouth close to her ear. 'I shall tell how you come, bringing the smells of the garden and feeling with finger and lips. I shall tell how Paddington Bear cannot guard me because against your magic he is too small. I shall tell that you are very bad because you pretend to be the king.' 'And whom shall you tell?' the voice breathed against her cheek. Boldly she answered, 'I shall tell the king. I shall tell the queen my mother. I shall tell the lady-in-waiting. I shall tell the women who launder our garments. I shall tell the cook.'

'I did try once,' Magdalen defended herself. 'I did try to stop it. Once, long ago.'

Then the monster said, still using the king's voice: 'You must tell no one. This is our secret. If you break it, you will pay the penalty. I have many in my store. Perhaps one day I shall take one out to show you. Then you will never again be tempted to disclose this secret that is special to us.'

The princess could not imagine what these penalties might be; she did not know precisely what 'penalty' meant, but she hoped that the monster would never take one out of his store to show her. As he told her about it, his arms had gripped her to him until it hurt.

You were so young then, Magdalen addressed the princess. You were hardly more than an infant. How could you confront his threats? And since they were made in the voice of authority, you had no choice but to obey.

But she wasn't young any longer. Last night, why couldn't she take control? Nowadays she knew the position. She knew the danger he flouts. Why couldn't she issue threats? She had no more strength against him than that haunted, deceived child. For his hold on her had tightened. Other feelings had been added to the fear. Would she be able to describe those when she came to them? Was it because of them that last night she had been unable to cry out: Let me alone?

She told herself aloud, 'You're a coward. You disgust me.'

The word ran down her body, touched her breasts, lingered in the dip of her navel, glided down her flanks and streamed from her thighs. And she was out of the bed, stripping off the sheet, the pillow case, was shaking the duvet from its cover while in her head she re-read Mrs Brook's note written two years earlier: 'I have washed the sheets you put out. Had you forgotten that you had already changed them this week? When I was looking for more, I found this old duvet cover. Fancy you having one printed with pictures of Paddington Bear! Do you want it or shall I take it to the Shelter shop? PS I'll put the cover away again if it's got sentimental attachments.'

She had torn up the note, dashed out and thrust the cover into the dustbin, pressing it upon a mess of fish scales and egg shells, into the stink of rotting cabbage leaves and unexamined slime. Next she had buried it, throwing spadesful of earth over it and, seeing a worm contract then burrow, she had rejoiced: 'And worms'll come and yeet thee up, on Il-l-k-le-ey Moor baht'attttt. Seen you off, Paddington Bear.'

This day, Magdalen screwed up the bed linen and kicked it under her dressing-table, groaning, 'I sicken myself. I've never gone any further than a few minor rebellions. All I do to defy him is take a shower.'

She was dried and about to leave the bathroom when her father said through the door, 'May I enter?'

'Sorry.'

'In that case, would you pack my toilet bag?'

Her pulse leapt. 'This is an early start.'

'There's no reason to delay.'

'I suppose not.'

In the mist on the mirror she drew a wide face; the mouth was a melon-slice grin. Already she anticipated his absence and thought: I could throw the party tonight.

'There's business I must attend to first. I forgot to mention something to Hustler and I've promised I'll drop in to see Leonie Dawson. Naturally I shall make that short. I should be back in ninety minutes or less. Be ready, won't you?'

His footsteps padded along the landing and down the stairs, then in the distance was the click of the side door. A few minutes later the engine of his car turned over, burst into accelerating noise, but Magdalen didn't hear it. She was trying to recall what her father had referred to when he had said: 'There's no reason to delay,' and, 'Be ready, won't you?' Gradually other words returned to her: 'Harley Gresham put me in touch with the accommodation wallah in Edinburgh.' They had finished dinner and her father was pricking a cigar. 'Apparently they can provide university accommodation for first-year undergraduates.' She had nodded, thinking: I'll let him finish before I tell him what I've decided to do. He had held his lighter at the optimum distance from the cigar, given a quick suck and checked the tobacco's glow. 'However, if we prefer we can make our own arrangements.' Tieing the belt of her bathrobe, Magdalen stopped; her fingers froze. 'So I've phoned a number of estate agents renting out or selling flats. We'll go tomorrow.' He had smiled at her, happy. 'You'll enjoy choosing.'

Once again he had achieved exactly what he wanted as easily as he had lit his cigar.

Immediately she had forgotten it. She had blocked it out. That did not surprise her. She was a professional at doing that. Now, the significance of his intention hit her like a punch in the groin and she bent over the hand basin, winded, gulping for breath. He meant to set her up in a flat, a place he could visit, but not like an overnight guest in a Hall of Residence or a Student House, subject to curious eyes. She would not be surrounded by students. There would be no friends running in and out of her room. She would be alone in a flat that was private; shut off, and he would stay at his convenience and be unobserved. She would be no safer in Edinburgh than she was here.

'Nothing's altered,' she whispered. 'Not a thing.'

All the glad hopes of the last months vanished. So short the time now seemed, so precious, when she had persuaded herself that by the autumn she would be free. If she could get to university. She had succeeded and he had sabotaged her plan. The work had been useless; the hope of escape was nothing more than an impractical dream. She had deceived herself; she had put her faith in a plan which had been doomed from the start. It was inevitable that he had the victory. She stared at the mirror, watched the grinning face in the steam break up, become striped by drips, and she moaned, 'He's more cunning than I am and he knows how to get what he wants; that's his job. However hard I try, I can't overcome that.'

There was no more she could do to fight him. She

could not break the silence of years. It was impossible to explain to anyone why she did not want to live in a flat he rented or bought. Their ears had been taught to receive only the smooth tones of her father; their eyes had been tricked to notice only what he wished. Nor could she dial the Rape Crisis number she had in her diary; she had tried once, had listened to the patient voice, while the handset slipped in her hand and her tongue would not move. Finally she had cancelled the call. She couldn't say the words.

He was too strong for her. Since the first night he had come to her, she had been in his control. She was paralysed by his power.

Magdalen dragged back to her bedroom and began to dress. She could bear it no longer. Not after she had worked so hard for the future and, for a few hours, had breathed in its promise. Only for it to be snatched away.

She looked round her. Food lay cold on a tray. Under the dressing-table there were pillow slips, a duvet cover crunched up. It would always be like this. It would be like this wherever she went. Magdalen looked into the future and saw only a repetition of the past.

'It's over,' she stated. 'I'm finished.'

The larger hand on her watch pointed to nine, the smaller to eight. Slowly she worked it out, then the sum: forty minutes before the mechanics at the garage arrived for work. She had time. She finished dressing and picked up her handbag. In it was the set of keys she had to open the filling station when she was on early shift. She walked out of the house and collected her bicycle.

At the petrol station she unlocked the office and disarmed the security system. She opened the cupboard where the car keys were kept and chose one of them. She walked into the repair shed, matched the key to the car, saw that only the bodywork appeared to be damaged but opened the bonnet and checked.

Then she examined the exhaust pipe and assessed the diameter of the rubber tubing that would fit.

Six

The next minutes were endless. The sun slanted through the door of the repair shed but the corners were in shadow. When she found some pieces of tubing they all seemed to be the wrong width or too short. At last she was satisfied and, returning to the car, she pushed one end of the tube over the pipe. Though it was secure, she decided that to keep it firmly in place she needed something to twist round it. Her eyes searched the shed, looking for wire; they picked out a figure standing at the door. It advanced towards her, at first slowly, then its pace quickened. A voice demanded, 'What the hell are you up to?'

She shouted back, 'Leave me alone!' As she should have shouted to him, her father, years before. But this man wasn't her father; he was the cousin of Melanie Howkins, Greg.

'Go away,' she shouted again, grabbed the end of the tube that lay coiled on the floor and, taking it in both hands, swung it full into his chest.

He stepped back, crossing his arms to protect his belly, and she lashed at his wrists, at his sides and shoulders, screeching, 'Leave me! Get out!' As she bore down upon him she heard the exhaust pipe rattle and behind her the tube sprang away. But her hands were still clenched over the whipping end of the tube.

Then he had caught it, was trying to wrench it from her and it was stretched out rigid between them. She saw its length snaking uselessly among the cars.

'Let go of it!' she screamed but Greg's grip was stronger than hers. Clinging to the tube, she was dragged on its leash, thrown against a pile of tyres that crashed down. There was a spray of fluid and the thud of a fallen can. The tyres rolled, hit her legs; oil spread under her. Her boots skidded. She heard a wing mirror snap and the grating of glass. Then there was a wheel arch above her head, a chassis embossed with mud and a bumper filled with rust that dripped brown flakes. Her hands were empty. She heard a high continuous shriek and the words, 'That's the last thing I need.'

The noise was the alarm of a car. Greg said, 'We'd better get out of here before anyone comes.'

He stretched down, pulled her up and eased her towards a wall. She leant against it. All her energy and resolution had gone. Her mind had been focused upon that piece of rubber tubing. Now it wasn't there. She watched Greg right the can of oil and collect the tyres. He fetched a brush and swept up the broken glass.

'Come on,' he said and steered her between the cars, through the repair shed and into the office. On the desk was her bag. Greg took it and the keys which lay beside it, led her out and locked the door. On the forecourt was Melanie's hatchback. 'Get in,' he ordered.

The clock on the dashboard read eight-twenty; by that time everything would have been completed if Greg hadn't interfered. She wanted to say, 'I hate you,' but she was too tired.

Shops, traffic, pedestrians crammed round her then slid behind as the car passed through the town, went over a bridge, turned and curved, stopped under trees. Greg left her. She watched him cross the road and step down a low bank. There was the splash of water.

She felt totally alone and this frightened her. Yet she didn't want anyone to be there. She heard someone walking over the suspension bridge and a man came, surrounded by busy dogs. 'Fine morning,' he greeted, and climbed over the stile into the woods. She stared after him, puzzled by his greeting; it had no connection with her.

When Greg returned, his face was wet and the hair on his forehead dripped. 'Mucky place, that repair shop,' he told her and dried himself with a duster he found. Through his door which was standing open she could see cars of commuters going past. After that, Greg came to her again with the duster soaked. 'Want to clean up? Ah well,' he answered her silence, 'river water's not a lot of good for removing oil,' and he placed the little mound of fabric in front of her on a ledge.

So much was going on, she was bewildered; she wished it were quiet and still. Greg was fiddling with the wrist bands of his sweat shirt; he was trying to wring them out; a young man had parked his motor cycle near them and was doing roadside maintenance. She closed her eyes but that didn't stop these things happening. A lorry went by them lifting the dust, then a tractor with a trailer that swayed. Later there was a line of faces high up in a touring coach. She did not belong to any of this; it was a picture slipping across a large screen and she was a stranger separated by an immense distance while against her wishes she was forced to look.

Greg was asking a question but she did not listen. 'Where?' he repeated.

She shook her head.

'Home?' He saw her recoil. 'You don't want me to take you home?'

'No!' The sound of her own voice startled her. It was dry and shrill. 'No!'

After a silence he said, 'I don't . . . what is . . . I mean, why? . . . this morning. You seemed fine yesterday evening.'

Yesterday evening. It flicked at her memory.

'I wouldn't have found you but I wanted to catch you before the filling station got busy.'

She wished he would stop talking.

'I hadn't heard, yesterday, the party was off. You'll know that, but I was hoping there was no aggro.'

The party. She could not give it her attention.

'Magdalen, please speak to me. Why were you doing it . . . in the petrol station . . . what got you to the point . . . this morning?'

She shook her head.

'I don't know what to do.'

His voice was plaintive, small as a child's, and his words echoed her own. They came from years earlier. But she had found something to do and she had done it. She remembered herself, a young girl, sitting with a dog in the back of a truck, hoping that soon it would reach the place the driver had promised and she would have a view of the sea. She said, 'You could take me to Collingham.'

'What, *now*?'

'It's near Wetherby.'

'But it's not half an hour since you were . . .'

'I'll get a hitch on the A1.' Then continue north.

'You can't do that!'

'Forget it.' She searched for her handbag, found it on the back seat.

'Look, you can't hitch, not now. You haven't any . . . any luggage.'

'That's not necessary.'

'You're covered in oil.' He pulled down the passenger mirror and she caught sight of a white oval smudged with dark streaks. 'You need to clean up. I mean, you can't hitch, looking like that.' His voice faltered. The conversation was ridiculous.

'Don't worry. I only asked.'

She knew now what she needed. She had to get to the sea. It had never failed her. Always it had renewed her strength. After she had been there she would be able to consider the future. Her hand reached to the latch of the door.

'Right, I'll consider it, but I'll have to nip back to Melanie to see if it's OK to borrow her car.'

'Thanks.'

Melanie Howkins was in her dressing-gown reading a

newspaper while she dipped into a tub of yoghurt. The tangy fragrance of coffee met them as Greg opened the door. 'Catch her?' Melanie asked him and finished the sentence she was reading before looking up. 'Whatever's happened?'

'Magdalen's slipped in some oil. Have you anything to clean it off?'

'I may have.' She searched in a cupboard and found detergent, a cloth. 'Come and sit down,' she told Magdalen and wiped the oil from her face. 'What a mess. Now your hands.' Obediently Magdalen held them out while the other scrubbed. 'There's a lot on your denims as well.'

'They'll wash.'

Magdalen waited, wishing the other two would finish their whispers. 'I can't believe it,' she heard Melanie say. 'This isn't the Magdalen I know. She's so balanced, together. And it's only two days since those marvellous results. Thank heaven you turned up. Reasons? No, I think it's too early, Greg, to ask questions.'

Magdalen wanted to shout: Hurry! She was miles away from the sea but the thought of it was bringing back some of the energy. The ache in her head was diminishing and her body was lighter. Only her stomach resisted. It was clenched by anxiety but she could not work out the cause.

There were other murmurs: 'She wants to get on to the A1. Hitch a lift,' and: 'We can't let her do that. Hitching lifts. At this moment. We'll have to think of something.'

She turned to Magdalen and said gently, 'I'll find you some clean clothes; we're about the same size.'

About to enter the bedroom, Melanie was stopped by the telephone's ring. 'This'll be Don,' she said, but the voice on the line was Lindsay Wilde's.

'I apologise for troubling you, Miss Howkins. I hope I'm not disturbing anything important.'

'Only a late breakfast.'

'I'm wondering whether Magdalen has been to see you this morning, to return your book.'

Glancing at his daughter, Melanie was astonished to see she had risen, her face white.

'Ah, that book I lent her.' She smothered the mouthpiece against her shoulder and asked Magdalen, 'Do you want to speak to your father?'

'No! Please!'

Melanie nodded. 'She hasn't returned it, Mr Wilde. As I mentioned yesterday evening, there's no hurry.'

'I suppose you couldn't suggest where she might be?'

'She could be here now. I think I can see someone at the door. Would you wait a moment?' She put her hand over the mouthpiece and asked, 'Magdalen, what shall I say?'

Magdalen clutched the back of her chair. This was the anxiety which had screwed into her stomach: that her father should catch her. She would not be able to withstand his questions, conceal from him what she had attempted this morning, and there would be retributions, penalties, revenge. He would probably drag her with him to the Netherlands, keep her under close watch, threaten to have her sectioned. She wavered. Why don't I give in and do what he wants? she thought. It would be easier.

But Melanie was waiting for her to answer and Magdalen said to herself: She's prepared to lie in order to shield me. So she whispered, grateful, 'I'm not here. He mustn't come.'

Again Melanie nodded. 'I'm sorry about that, Mr Wilde. It wasn't Magdalen after all. Someone was calling at my neighbour's. Now, what was your question?'

It was repeated. Lindsay Wilde's tone was suspicious.

'I'm afraid it's unlikely I should know where she is. I'm not her mate, merely her Physics mistress, or was. Isn't she working at the Moor petrol station?'

'I've checked there, although she shouldn't be going in this morning. Other plans have been made. I'm rather worried, Miss Howkins. You may not know this, but Magdalen can be unpredictable at times. She can get it into her head to do some strange things. And these last months have been a strain, so much hard work, then the excitement of the results.'

'I thought she coped rather well.'

'I'm relieved to hear you say that. Perhaps her friend Gail will be able to help.'

Why haven't I any sympathy with this man? Melanie thought. 'I don't suppose your daughter mentions every-thing she's going to do, and it's only a quarter-past nine.'

'That's the time I asked her to be ready to leave.'

'In that case I'm sure she'll be home soon. Now, you must excuse me. I have to take my car to a garage for its MOT.'

Replacing the handset, she asked, 'You heard that, Magdalen?'

'Yes.'

'I'd appreciate a cup of coffee, Greg. I think we all would.'

As he handed one to Magdalen he remembered what she had said the day before: What I most want is to get away; I don't only mean from home.

'Take heart,' he encouraged, and steadied her rattling cup.

'He'll start searching for me. I've got to go.'

Melanie did not need to be prompted. She had been told that Lindsay Wilde was respected, a man with charisma and charm, though she herself had seen little of that the previous evening. He was, according to the head-master, a devoted parent. Yet his daughter was terrified of him. Two days ago she had learnt that she had excellent grades and that a university place was confirmed; this morning she had attempted to take her own life. Now she sat in Melanie's kitchen desperate that her father might find her. A woman shaking with fear.

Magdalen knows what's best for her at the moment: to get away, Melanie said to herself. But she can't be left alone; we have to prevent her from trying to commit suicide again.

To Magdalen, she said, 'Greg tells me you want to get on to the A1.'

The other nodded.

Melanie recalled Harley Gresham saying, 'She'd disappear, make for the coast, favoured Northumbria for some reason.'

'I see. Well, Greg's prepared to take you. He can

borrow my car.' Then she became brisk, purposeful. 'You'd better collect some food, Greg,' she told him. 'There's fruit, biscuits. You'll find cheese and apple juice in the fridge; take anything else you think might be useful. We'll get you changed, Magdalen, and put a few clothes together.'

Ten minutes later she said at the car, 'You'll need money.'

'I've got some.'

'All the same, Greg had better have this.' She handed him a cash card and made him recite the PIN number. 'If you forget it, give me a ring; and you can keep the car as long as you like. If I need one, I'll borrow Donald's.'

'What about the MOT?'

'Oh, Greg!' She laughed, gave him a sudden hug. 'You're so innocent. If the damned thing is in for its MOT, there's less risk it'll be searched for, isn't there? When you're dealing with a suspicious person, you have to be a move ahead. Now let Magdalen lie on the back seat and drape this rug over her.'

'Mel, you don't have to go over the top on the tricky stuff.'

Her face sobered. 'I should do it,' she advised Magdalen and watched as the other carried out her instruction. 'I'm fond of that rug. Came from my gran's. Used it on my bed before I could afford a duvet.' She held her dressing-gown against the light draughts as she leant into the car. 'I don't know what this is all about but you must've been in a pretty bad state. I hope you begin to feel better when you've got more space. Greg'll be with you. He's not a bad chap. Rotten at physics or anything mechanical,' she encouraged Magdalen to smile, 'but despite that he manages to muddle along. Have a safe journey.'

She said to Greg, low so that Magdalen should not hear: 'Look after her. No hitching. You must stay with her. Yes, I expect you mean to. We can't have a repeat of what she tried to do this morning.' Then she stood unwaving as he drove away.

Magdalen curled under the rug and, exhausted, immediately slept.

Seven

The clang of metal against metal and the loud pulse of a machine woke her. Through the window Greg's face leered and his mouth asked, 'Recognise it?' To give her a clue, he jerked the nozzle out of the petrol tank and waved it like a flag. A jet of petrol curved into the air and dropped, most on himself. She heard him curse and watched him mop up. Amused, she thrust the rug aside and climbed out of the car, then she found she was giggling loudly and could not stop. A woman at the next pump tutted disapproval.

It was still morning. A clock on the forecourt read eleven thirty-three. I must break this habit of stating time at the exact minute, as Dad does, she told herself. Why can't I simply say: A little after half-past eleven? Or: Nearly four hours since I left home, since I . . . For a moment her thoughts jumped back, spun among half-repaired cars, through a sludge of spilled oil and a strange tug of war. It was unreal. There had been a reason but she would not think about that, not yet. It should not be too difficult to find distraction, to occupy her mind with other things.

Greg had succeeded in jamming the cap of the tank; his

hands were stippled with petrol. Yes, she would take things as they came, one at a time. If she could. For the moment she had to stick the rest on the back burner.

She was aching after being cramped in the back of the car. Magdalen stretched and rolled up the sleeves of Melanie's shirt. It was another sun-glittering day. Melanie had been right about finding some space. There was plenty where she was going. Soon she would be there.

'Whereabouts are we?' she asked Greg when he returned from paying for the petrol. The filling station was a small parochial affair; the road beside it ran between hedges; nailed to a tree was a hand-written poster advertising a garden fête; in the distance an engine started up but no vehicle came. 'This isn't the A1.'

'No. I can't say exactly where we are. I didn't like the look of the signs to Durham and Newcastle at Scotch Corner so I bore left. You want to go north so I'm keeping in the right direction.'

How could anyone be so hopeless? And she had been landed with him for a chauffeur. 'I don't suppose you've noticed the road number? You know, on the signposts, as you tootled along?'

'I'm afraid not, but we're pointing to West Auckland.'

'That's miles out.'

'I'm sorry but, you see, you don't need to get a lift on the A1. I can take you the whole way.'

So that was his reason. He had decided to keep an eye on her and he wanted to prevent her from hitching. He wasn't so much her chauffeur as her chaperon.

'Don't worry about me. It'll be no bother,' he assured

her. 'I like driving and I'm not rushed for time.'

'Well, I am,' she snapped. She was losing her patience. He was delaying the sight of the sea. 'If you take me up to Consett, then Corbridge, I'll get a lift on the A69 to Newcastle and back on to the A1.'

He sighed. 'You certainly know your way about.'

'I know this one.' The first time she had run out of the house with nothing, not even an anorak. The driver of the van had been kindly and worried; she was the same age as his daughter and he had been shocked at the thought of his child running away. He had taken her into a café, bought her a plate of chips, said he was going to the lavatory, and telephoned the police. The next time she got further; she had been into the library, had made tracings of maps, had learnt the road numbers, the towns, had saved up, had a story ready: that she had lost her coach ticket. But on the third day she was caught, like a criminal, by a stout woman with a portable phone, gripping her wrists. It was not until the fourth occasion that her escort, another woman, with bigger hands but less stout, told her that her father engaged private investigators. This one had tried to pretend she was not a wardress; she had kept her big hands in her pockets and had said, 'You can have another run along the beach before we go. If that's what you came for, why don't you ask your pa? He'd bring you.'

She had answered, 'I don't want him to bring me. I don't want him ever, ever to come here.'

Shocked, her keeper had answered, 'I don't see why not. He's a lovely chap, your dad is, and worried sick about you.'

Greg asked, 'Where are you going?'

She saw the wide stretch of sand, the plashes of water holding the light, the waves folding, cleaning as they ebbed. She did not wish him to go there; it was not a place to be shared.

So she shrugged. 'I'll tell you when I see it.'

'I imagined there was someone. Someone you wanted to meet.' He was almost stammering. 'I thought your parents were . . . were separated, divorced.'

She was touched by his shyness. 'There isn't anyone. My mother is dead.'

'I'm sorry.'

'No problem, Greg. She died when I was a kid. Of leukaemia. To tell you the truth, I can hardly remember her. She spent a lot of time in bed, because of the illness, I suppose. I was always looked after by somebody else.' That was all there was to say about it, Magdalen told herself and, climbing into the car, she returned to her previous seat.

The princess was sitting in her dressing-gown eating her breakfast when suddenly the queen's breath puffed out and she bent over a chair. She called to her lady-in-waiting, 'Please telephone the king and see that the princess is washed and attired in fresh garments.' However, when the dressing was finished the queen did not adjust the folds of her robe and stroke the ribbon in the princess's hair because she was lying on her couch, watching her lady-in-waiting who was laying silken apparel in a soft leather case. The king came and carried the queen down the stairs. 'We shall not be long,' he promised the princess as he arranged the queen on his horse. 'Where are you going?' she asked him. 'We are going to the surgery, to fetch medicines. The women of the castle are busy but I have ordered the gardener to keep an eye on you.' The princess declared that she wished to go with them and she clung to the king's leg but he lifted her aside, kicked his steed and bore the queen away. He looked very solemn. A king heavy with cares.

The gardener came to pull up the drawbridge. He said to her, 'Now you be careful. I'm watching,' and he brought out a hoe. The princess ran away and hid in one of the greenhouses but, when the gardener found her, he did not rebuke her for wriggling behind his chrysanthemums and bending their stalks. He did not say, 'If I were your father,' and frown. Such a threat was unnecessary. He had a monster to do his punishing work. Nor did he repeat what he had once made his monster say to her:

'You must tell it to no one. This is our secret. If you break it, you will pay the penalty. I have many in my store. Perhaps one day I shall take one out to show you. Then you will never be tempted again to disclose this secret that is special to us.'

He did not bother to remind her of that terrible threat because she would soon see it at work.

For, in order that she should appreciate the kind of punishment she could receive if she told anyone their secret, the gardener had instructed the monster to take one of his penalties out of his store. And that morning, the one he had taken out was to make the queen die.

However, it was a long time before the princess understood.

The king returned to the castle and, holding her hand, he explained that the queen was to take her medicines in hospital. The gardener commiserated; he was sly and cunning and easily concealed what he had done.

In the days that followed, the king pushed the princess on her swing and played with her in her sand-pit; he took her for walks in the park and bought her ice-cream; he put her behind him on his great snorting horse and rode to the fair; at the fair he fired a gun at pictures and won a coconut. In the evenings he let her splash him in her bath, dusted her all over with a great powder-puff and carried her to bed. Through all these days he did not ride out to his kingdom but sent messages to tell his people what they must do. He looked worried and pale but every night, sitting by her bed until she fell asleep, he also looked fierce. Therefore seeing the king's face, so hard and determined, the monster did not visit her. He did not dare.

The princess enjoyed having the king to play with but somehow the days were not right when the queen was not there and every morning she asked when she would return. The king could not tell her, which was puzzling since he always had the answer to questions, but he said, 'She has been asking to see you, so I will take you today.'

The queen was in a room all by herself. At her bedside was a table with vases of flowers on it and a great many cards. The people who had sent them had made a mistake, the princess thought, because it wasn't the queen's birthday. There was a bottle on a hook with a transparent tube hanging from it that went under the sheet. She could not reach the queen where her head lay on the pillow so the king lifted her up to kiss. 'I like your new dress,' the queen said. The words wheezed in her throat. 'It's got sixteen buttons,' the princess told her. 'Let me see them.' The princess twirled round and waited until the queen had counted. It took her a long time. When the princess turned, the queen was looking at the king who had his handkerchief out and was holding it to his face. 'I think that's enough,' the nurse said at the door. She bent down to the princess and told her: 'I like your dress. Can you make it spin out?' 'I've dusted your dressing-table,' the princess told the queen, 'and I've put your lipstick in the drawer so you know where it is when you come back.' Courteously the queen thanked her. Then, 'Goodbye,' she said. 'Look after the king for me, won't you?'

After the queen died many people visited the castle. They talked with the king in the great chamber and the princess was sent out to play. She

71

walked along the paths and round the pond hoping that the gardener would not notice her but he was standing at the top of the steps that led down to the black door. He said, pretending to be kind, 'Do you want a look?' She shook her head and ran away but he had seen she was crying and strode after her. When he had caught her, he found her handkerchief in her pocket and dabbed at her cheeks. 'Don't take on,' he told her. His hands smelt of soil and the horse plop he put on the roses. 'She was ailing. I reckon she was glad to go. Your father's a good man. He'll see you don't want. Won't you stop these tears? Your mother wouldn't like to see them. She'd want you to be happy and smile at your dad. And you will, won't you? I expect you'll be a good girl now.'

When she heard that, the princess fled into the castle. She climbed up to her turret, squeezed behind a sofa and hid. 'What are you doing there?' they asked her and she was taken down to the kitchen where the cook placed food before her, but she pushed it away. The lady-in-waiting said, 'I will stay the night and sleep with her in her bed.'

The next day and for many days after the princess was surrounded by voices. One said, 'She's hardly eating. I tempt her with all her favourite dishes but she won't touch them. All I succeed with is cheese and a slice of dry toast.' Another asked, 'Have you seen her colouring book? She's filled it with scribbles.' A third one explained, 'I can't persuade her to play in the garden. She hides behind the sofa and won't come out.' Then together the voices chanted, 'She's grieving. It's affecting her more than was expected. She's spent more time with the lady-in-waiting than she has with the queen. Joanna has done the mothering. Even so, you can't discount the shock. The child must miss her mother. We didn't altogether approve of that visit to the hospital. Not, in our opinion, the right place to see her mother for the last time. Perhaps the child is thinking about that. Children are a mystery. You can never know what is going on inside their little heads.'

They were right. They hadn't the slightest notion. Inside the head of the princess was the fact that the queen her mother had gone and it was the gardener's monster who had sent her away. Inside her head the gardener was speaking: 'Your mother was ailing. I reckon she was glad to go. I know you'll be a good girl now.' He was telling her that she would be good because now she had seen the power of his magic. His monster had shown her one of the penalties he kept in his store: he had made the queen ail and got her dead.

The princess thought: Perhaps, if I'm very good, he will let her come back. Therefore she ate all the food that was prepared for her, wiping her plate clean with a piece of bread till it shone; she scrubbed her teeth until the bristles of the brush bent over; she never threw her ball into the flower-beds or broke off a rose. So, every morning the princess woke up and said to herself: Today he will bring her home. But when she ran down to breakfast the queen was not there. The princess sighed, disappointed. She'll come tomorrow, she assured herself, and felt more cheerful.

Thus the days passed. The sun warmed the water in the paddling pool; in the quiet nights she slept in the crook of the Joanna's arm; no longer did voices chant round her and the words of the gardener vanished out of her head. Then one day after the king had climbed upon Merk his charger and gone to rule his people, the princess stopped outside the door of the royal chamber, opened it and tiptoed inside. It looked just the same as it had always done except that the queen's slippers were not on the furry rug and her make-up had been removed. The lipstick that the princess had placed in a drawer remained, however, as she had left it in a nest of cotton wool. That meant it was ready if the queen should return. 'I bet she'd be cross,' the princess exclaimed. 'She never got grumpy if I woke her with my noise; she never frowned, Now you be careful, I'm watching; she never said she'd a Something for chasing naughty girls. But I bet she'd be cross with that gardener. I bet, if she knew, she'd put him across her knee, drop his bloomers and take a slipper to his bottom till he couldn't sit down.' The princess laughed at the picture of this and pranced round the chamber, tipsy with revenge.

In that jolly mood she decided to dust the queen's

dressing-table. She had not done that for a very long time. She fetched a clean duster from the kitchen, climbed on the stool, screwed the duster into a wad, blew on the surface of the dressing-table and began to rub. 'She wouldn't say I'm to blame,' she explained to it. 'She wouldn't say I need a spank. She knows I've been good so that she can come back. She wouldn't blame me. She'd say it's the gardener's fault she's deaded.' The princess lilted and crooned the words, sending them round with the duster, polishing a charm ring upon the bright wood. Until gradually something stirred under the gleaming surface. She saw arms stretched up to embrace and a smile on the mouth. The lips moved and the princess laid her ear inside the circle and listened.

'Magdalen, are you ill?' She understood that Greg was speaking, addressing her reflection in the driving mirror.

He repeated, 'Are you ill?'

'No, I don't think so. Do you want me to check?'

'Yeah, do that. It's the lip movements I'm particularly worried about. Is there such a condition as chronic labial hyperactivity? That is, without using the voice.'

'I don't know.'

'You're the medic.'

'Not quite yet, but watch this space. I was thinking.'

'Is that what happens when you *think*?'

'I've no idea. I've never watched myself.'

'It's worse than somebody mouthing the words while he reads.'

'Could you make any of it out?'

'I didn't try.'

'I'm cobbling together my memories of something. I suppose I could go on writing it down.'

'I wish you would.'

'It's not for anyone to read.'

'I hope not. It gives me the creeps.'

She opened her handbag; the notebook had not been removed the previous night. Magdalen was not sure that she wished to continue this story. It was hard either to think it or write, although the form she had chosen provided a little protection. It made her task a shade easier than coming straight out with the word.

She riffled through the pages, left a blank to insert the section she had thought out, should she remember it accurately, then continued:

So it was that the princess saw the queen's face in the gleam of the dressing-table and her arms stretched to hold her. This meant that although the gardener's monster had taken her away he could not stop her ghost coming back. Because she was sure that the queen could not rise out of the dressing-table, the princess was not alarmed and she was glad that the queen was there. She thought there was a sound, a frail echo of something she had once heard. She held her breath and, pressing her ear to the woman's mouth, she felt the flittering touch of the queen's moth voice. Gradually she heard words being spoken. They were the queen's last request.

'Look after the king for me,' the queen said. 'I will,' the princess promised.

She did not know how to do it. She could not cook dishes for him, clean his chamber or wash his fine raiment. But she decided that these duties were not what the queen intended. She had cherished him in other ways. Therefore the princess tried to follow the queen her mother's example. Each morning she arranged his post in a neat pile; she asked the woman in charge of the laundry to make sure that his shirts were ironed; she answered the telephone for him, memorised the messages exactly, and recited them to him when he returned home. This pleased the king greatly. He told his people that he had found another Personal Assistant and that she was worth her weight in gold. The ministrations of the princess did not end there, however. She remembered how the queen had hugged and kissed him. That, too, was a way of looking after him. Long ago the princess had often done that but she had been less inclined to after the monster had borrowed the king's voice. Now she returned to her former loving. He had missed it and she had much to make up.

The king would sit by her bed as he had done before the queen left them. He would hold her hand and say that she was his Precious. Sometimes he brought her a rose. But though she would have liked to confide in him, the princess did not describe how she could burnish the queen to appear in the gleam of the dressing-table. If she did, she thought that the monster would find out and she knew that would not please him. He would be angry if he learnt that a piece of the queen remained.

Not long after the princess heard the queen's last request and she had become the king's Personal Assistant, the monster returned. This distressed the princess greatly; she had believed his visits were over. She no longer spoilt the lawns with her tricycle; she had taken it to the stable and hidden it from view. Therefore she could not puzzle out why her punishment had been renewed. But she did not protest; she kept quiet. Nor did she ever consider revealing their secret; she knew now precisely what the monster meant by 'penalty' and she was trapped by his magic power.

Magdalen paused and thought: All these reasons I worked out for what was happening! I know I've got them right yet I'm amazed that the truth didn't click sooner. But it's hindsight that makes me say that. I was a high-spirited child but trained to be obedient, and I loved Dad. Was it surprising that the truth should be slow in coming to me? I think I half knew it but I blocked it out. It *had* to be magic. It *had* to be a monster sent by Mr Hustler. If it wasn't, I was lost.

She had to shut away the possibility that the person who clothed her, fed her, played with her, who was perfect, a shining god, could betray her trust in him and do her harm.

The princess was trapped. So she complied with the monster's desires, closing her thoughts to his fingers and drubbing tongue. When he told her that she was a good girl, kind to him and loving, she would hold back her tears. And afterwards, remembering the queen's wish, she would comfort him as he sobbed in the darkness. Those were the nights when the king lent the monster his voice.

Magdalen stopped writing and read the last paragraph. Her eyelids were hot but they remained dry. She despised him now for those tears and refused to be associated with them. Somewhere, in the pit of her belly, behind the cage-bars of her ribs, something flickered. It was a quiet anger budding through the disgust.

Eight

'Magdalen, are you hungry?' Greg's voice roused her.

'I haven't noticed. No.'

'I am.'

'Didn't you bring some stuff?'

'I've eaten an apple and a packet of biscuits but they've worn off. You use up a lot of energy at the wheel of this space bug.'

'How much further have we to go?'

He could have said: If you told me where we are going I might be able to answer. Instead, he reminded himself that he had to be patient. 'We've gone past Consett.'

'Yes.' There had been a bend, a sudden descent, a bridge, trees and through them the sparkle of water.

'Look, I think we should stop,' he said as they passed a sign advertising bar meals. 'Let's see what's on offer.'

'Do we have to? Can't you wait?' She had to keep moving. She had to reach her goal. Nothing else mattered. 'Greg, I'm not hungry.'

He did not answer. They had come to the public house and he had drawn in and was concentrating upon parking.

He can afford to ignore me; it's his car, he's the driver, she said to herself. He's the one in charge. I shouldn't have let myself get into this position. She was agitated by the delay. She had no interest in food. Her only need, urgent, compelling, was to reach the waiting sea.

'Come on.' Greg got out of the car. 'I'm starving and you could do with something to eat. Set you up.'

As he spoke, a lorry pulled in, the driver rolled down his window and called, 'Any idea how I get to Alnwick, mate?'

'Alnwick?' Greg began. 'Isn't that north of . . .' but Magdalen answered, 'I'll show you,' and ran round to the passenger side.

Greg followed her, heard her say, 'I'll direct you if you'll give me a lift,' and the lorry driver answer, 'Suits me. Jump in. Give that door a good yank; the lock sticks.'

Then Greg had his arms round her waist, was telling her: 'No, you don't,' and she was shouting, 'Let me go,' was wrestling with the handle, and the driver was leaning over the passenger seat, cautioning, 'Take it easy. What's going on?'

'She doesn't need a lift.' Greg had to raise his voice because the window was only half open and Magdalen was clawing at the door, yelling, 'Let me alone.' But he was pulling her away, gripping her tightly, attempting to latch a foot round her ankle while she twisted against him. Over the bonnet of the lorry he could see a group of people watching from the public house.

He gasped out, 'Try making for Corbridge.' He was grappling with Magdalen, struggling to hold her back, but she lunged forward and he saw the man recoil, incredulous, and heard him let out the clutch as Magdalen tripped and went down.

'What did you . . .?' She scrambled to her feet. 'Do that for?'

'What about you?'

'Stopping me.'

They were both panting. The lorry was turning out of the car park, its tyres screaming.

'Trying to dump me for another driver.'

'Was giving me a lift.'

'You already had one.'

'Not any more.'

She walked away from him and stood by the road. It was empty. Had she not been taught to suppress her feelings, she would have wept. She heard footsteps behind her and swung round, accusing, 'You're as bad as my father.'

'What makes you say that?'

'It's always his say-so that matters. What I want doesn't count.'

'It's counted all morning.'

'He'd say the same. He'd say I can have anything, anything I want.'

'Doesn't sound so bad. He'd have let you jump into that lorry, would he? Waved you off?'

'He wouldn't have made a scene in public.'

'The one yesterday evening was more discreet, yeah. But it had potential.'

'He wouldn't have dragged me out of the car if I'd jumped in when you asked me to the party.'

'In that case, it's a pity you didn't.'

'Since it was you issuing the invitation, I'm glad I didn't.'

'There wasn't one.'

'One what?'

'A party. And now you've brought it up, I'd like to mention that I've never cancelled a party someone else has arranged.'

She flinched and Greg cautioned himself: Watch it! Because she compares you with her dad, you aren't obliged to leap in and contradict. Keep out of the battle zone. They've got high explosives in there. No place for you pissing around with a water pistol.

'You don't hesitate to stop someone taking a lift when it's been offered,' she contrived to sneer.

But they were both aware that the argument had become childish, a playground squabble, and Greg said, conciliatory, 'I reckon the lorry driver went right off the idea when you started hammering on the door of his little cab.'

Remembering the driver's face, the hands flapping behind the glass, she smiled.

'Look, you don't have to keep an eye on the road, do you, Magdalen? It won't sneak away. I need to eat, have a sandwich. Won't you join me?'

'Can we make it quick?'

'I don't think we'll have any option. Our stock'll be low with the landlord. He doesn't hold with fighting in his car park and we lost him a customer.'

The fight had been seen by most of the people drinking

in the bar and they watched, curious, as Magdalen and Greg entered. The barman listened to their order without enthusiasm but at the sight of cash he risked a remark. 'You seem to be having a little difference of opinion.'

Greg shrugged. 'Just practising.'

'I'd like to see you on match form.'

'You could yet.'

'You're enjoying this,' Magdalen said, walking with him to a table.

'I'd have preferred not to have the tussle in the first place.'

'I wish they'd hurry up.'

'It's only three minutes since I ordered.'

'I don't know why you had to decide on hamburger and chips.'

'I bet it doesn't take longer than your sandwich. Can't you relax?'

'Not when I'm feeling held up.'

'We'll be out within thirty minutes. When you arrive there, wherever it is, you'll be in a pretty limp state if you've not had any food.'

'I'm not hungry.'

Greg told her about this three months later. 'You'd pretended you weren't hungry and you got through a sandwich as wide as a dinner plate and three storeys high.'

'Did I? I don't remember. Sounds revolting, not half as delicious as this. Try it.' She fished into the tall sundae glass piled with three flavours of ice-cream and popped a spoonful into his mouth.

But on that day, as they sat at a table in the bar of a

public house, they ate rapidly and without relish.

'Twenty-four minutes,' Frank calculated as they walked out. 'Must be a record. I hope it's worth the indigestion.'

Magdalen answered, 'Isn't that bloody! Look at that tyre.'

'They're having another spot of bother,' a customer in the bar reported. 'A flat.'

Greg said, 'I don't know whether Melanie belongs to one of those rescue services. There's no badge stuck anywhere.'

'You don't fetch someone out to change a wheel. Will you open the boot? We need the jack.'

Before she placed it under the wheel arch and raised the car, she asked, 'Will you have a go at loosening these nuts, please? You've got a stronger grip.'

He did this then continued as she instructed. Nodding towards their audience, he puffed, 'I bet they've never had such an enjoyable lunch-time drink. We'll go down in this pub's history. Why couldn't we simply blow the tyre up?'

'It's got a puncture.'

'You know, Magdalen, I've decided there are some skills I'm happy to be without,' he told her when the job was finished and the jack and punctured wheel stowed away.

'You'll have to drive carefully till we reach a garage. This spare is very low on air.'

'I'm relieved you don't suggest mouth to mouth resuscitation.'

The first petrol station they came to had no air machine

and the next, which had one, was a good distance further. The period of slow, cautious driving hampered their progress and the afternoon was almost over before Greg said, indicating trees to their left, 'Rothbury Forest, I think. Do we push on?'

'Please.' Before her in her mind was the sand firm and coldly wet, set into scallops by the drag of the receding waves.

But that night she did not reach it. It was already twilight when Greg drew into the grass verge and said, 'We're beyond Alnwick.'

She had been dozing and had hardly noticed the country they drove through; she recalled only the fairy-tale and the patches of exhausted sleep. She had pulled down the shutters on how the day had started, on what she had attempted, and why she had fled.

Greg was explaining, 'I don't think I want to drive any more. We'll find somewhere to sleep overnight.'

'I don't mind dossing down in the car.'

'Sorry; I need a bath. So do you.'

'You're always saying I ought to wash.'

'I'm surprised you don't feel dirty.'

'But I do. All the time.' The answer sprang out without her permission. The word dirty was always present; it lived on her skin.

Afterwards the princess would tiptoe into the bath chamber and try to wash away what the monster had left. Then she would dry herself and sprinkle the powder until she was pure again, covered with this soft unblemished snow. But that was an illusion. However much she washed, however much she powdered, the snail tracks of the monster remained.

Magdalen could see Greg frowning as he reflected upon her answer. I couldn't bear it, she said to herself, if he guessed.

Aloud, she added, trying to be bright, 'You feel dirty, you see, when you have rashes, eczema and so forth. That's what I meant.' She congratulated herself on the speed at which she could produce a lie to save a situation.

'I hadn't noticed.'

'It comes and goes. I was exaggerating when I said, all the time. Anyway, you're right about a bath.'

'Keep your eyes open, then, for a place to stop. Is a bed and breakfast OK?'

'That's fine.'

Since it was the peak holiday season, boards advertising bed and breakfast had a sign attached which read FULL, but after a few miles they saw B&B painted in whitewash on a gate. Looped over the post was a notice, VACANCIES.

'This looks more promising.' Greg turned down the track. 'I hope we're lucky. Today's been a day and a half. I haven't let up since early morning.' He paused, embarrassed by his reference to what she had done. 'The last time I stopped for petrol I bought some sandwiches and as soon as I've scoffed mine I intend to bathe and hit the sack.'

Hit the sack. The car became suffocating; the handle of the window slipped in her damp fingers as she tried to wind it down.

Breathless, she told him, 'I'm not going to share.'

'I wouldn't dream of it,' he snapped. 'Don't imagine I'm looking for lodgings with the sole thought of getting you into bed.' His speech was uneven, jerked by the car as it bumped along the track.

'It was something I had to say,' she defended.

'I disagree.'

'I had to make the position clear.'

'Hell! Where're you coming from? You seem to assume that all men are after the same thing.'

She wanted to say: It's enough that one is.

'In any case,' he continued, 'I've known you only a day.'

'But it's felt like one and a half.'

'The last two minutes have added another.' Self-mocking, he added, 'Listen to us! Like a couple of silly kids.'

'Kids aren't silly.'

'True.'

The track brought them to a bungalow, its walls painted planks, its roof a greying asphalt.

'Want to try it?'

Magdalen nodded. Once someone had attempted to make a garden and then lost interest but the flowers that survived had adjusted to weeds and the invading plants. Campanula formed tussocks over the stitching buttercups; white Michaelmas daisies bordered a patch of nettles; pansies straggled through feverfew; a poppy dropped tissue petals over lunaria's silver disks. There were no roses. 'It's nice,' she told him. As she climbed out of the car, a breeze brought her brine skimmed from the nearby sea.

'We've no one booked in tonight,' the owner told them at the door, 'but I'm sorry to say we can only do breakfast. We can't offer an evening meal. The wife's on night shift over at the hospital and I'm going out.' Seeing their rucksack, he approved, 'I always dreamed of travelling light myself, but the wife'd take the lot. Now you make yourselves at home and the local's only a step down the road. They do a nice chicken in a basket with chips. In the meantime, I'll brew you a pot of tea and put a plate of biscuits and such out in the kitchen. Help yourselves.' To Greg's question whether he could take a shower, he answered, 'There's hot water in plenty. You're more than welcome.'

They sat in the kitchen, drank the tea and ate biscuits and scones. The bungalow was cool and quiet. Outside a rabbit bobbed, nibbled and sniffed.

'I like it here,' Greg said. 'It's relaxing.'

She nodded, trying to suppress the apprehension. The owners of the bungalow were absent; she had been left alone with this man. She told herself: You're foolish; nothing will happen; he wishes you no hurt. But lifting his cup, Greg did not crook a finger through the ear but held it in his palm like a glass, and he rotated it before he drank as if he were warming a measure of brandy. And he was looking at her, examining her hair, asking whether she had always worn it so short, whether she had ever let it grow really long. And he was smiling. At any moment, he would say the words.

'I think I'll take that shower,' he told her.

Magdalen sat on her bed, waiting as she had always done. There was a thud of a shoe on the carpet then she heard him limping round the bedroom, one foot still shod, while he opened his wardrobe and drawers. The second shoe crashed against the skirting board and the springs of the bed creaked. Tonight he was humming, clearly in a good mood but in no hurry. The catch of the window clicked and the humming changed, became infinitesimally softer as he looked out. Eventually he closed the window, padded across the room barefoot and slipped through the door. At hers he stopped, his fingertips played a merry little arpeggio on the panel and he whispered, 'Shan't be long.' A few seconds later there were the clicks of switches, the buzz of a shaver, water drumming in the shower. Breath snuffled, was sneezed out and the water dripped and ceased. There followed the crack of a shaken towel, slaps as hands spread lotions upon neck and chest. The bathroom door opened. Footsteps approached her room. A voice murmured, 'All yours now, Magdalen. Good-night,' and the steps passed on. In the next room the bed took the weight of the man again; she heard him yawn.

For a long time Magdalen remained where she was sitting. She did not move. She looked at the furniture round her, at the chair with a faded cushion, at the bedhead upholstered in plastic, at the chest painted a garish yellow and the pink worn carpet. She examined them, disbelieving. They were not hers. They were not smart or luxurious; they had not been bought for her as bribes or rewards for being good. And she was not surrounded by walls that were built of stone. These were flimsy, constructed of thin wooden planks. It would be easy to hack them down or to find a crack through which, one by one, you could blow all the secrets.

Fumbling, commanded by fatigue, Magdalen undressed and lay down. She would wash later. Tonight there was no need. Inside these walls, feet did not stop at your door and enter after a shower had been taken. And no rose was placed in a vase by your bed.

Nine

Sometime in the middle of the night Magdalen was disturbed by a noise. Before she was fully awake, her body had stiffened and she had drawn the blankets tight over her breasts. She listened, expecting that any moment her ears would be attuned to the sounds she expected; but gradually she recalled where she was: in a room in a wooden bungalow, far away from the habits of home. And these sounds also were different, new. They did not match the others. Then her muscles loosened. What she heard was snores.

They droned on, tedious and insistent, but they did not exasperate her. She did not wish them to stop. Instead, she found a comfortable position and lay luxuriating in them. They were natural, made by a healthy, tired man. She whispered to herself: Could anyone appreciate how I long for such ordinary things? How this snoring can make me feel safe? Occasionally it did when I was a child. Something I had forgotten.

As her mind turned to sleep again, she thought the next paragraph.

One day the king told the princess that she was old

enough to set out from the castle and learn her lessons. She did not wish to do this; she wanted to stay with her lady-in-waiting but the king told her she could not. He spoke in a voice that sounded like the voice of the monster, therefore the princess grumbled no more. Every day she followed the king to the stable, was placed on Merk whose shining coat had been freshly groomed by the gardener and she was carried to school. It did not take her long to get used to it. The teachers were kind to her and she was put to sit next to a little girl who said, 'I'm Delia Williams. Who are you?' and soon the two became friends. Often when the school day was over the princess would return with Delia to her house and play. Delia's house was not as big as the castle and all it had at the back was a very small lawn splashed over with daisies. Delia's father said he liked daisies. Therefore the lawn was not cut and there wasn't a gardener. That made the princess glad. Then she decided that she should return Delia's hospitality. She wanted to show her friend round the place where she lived, just as Delia had. Thus it was arranged that Delia have tea with the princess one Saturday and that she should stay there that night.

It was a marvellous occasion. The cook made a trifle and little cakes with icing and chocolate truffles. The king took skewers and pierced them through chunks of sausages, tomatoes and green peppers, then he cooked them on a barbecue he had set up. When they had eaten he filled her paddling pool for them and afterwards he chased them into the castle where they all played blind man's buff. At bedtime the cook left the kitchen, saw that their teeth were brushed, and tucked them up in bed. The princess considered that there had never been a day like it. And that was not all. The night was even better because the monster did not come.

The princess was roused in the darkness but not by the smells of the garden or a goose-pimpling touch. She was woken by Delia snoring. This told the monster that there was someone in her chamber who would hear him however quietly he spoke. Delia's snores kept the monster away. The princess smiled that the monster was banished, and her sleep was not broken by prying fingers or filled by threatening dreams.

Next morning she was overjoyed to have someone at last to protect her and she begged the king to let Delia stay. He answered, 'She has to return to her cottage. Her mother and father would not wish her to live here for ever.' This was a great disappointment and the princess had to be satisfied with his promise that Delia could come again.

She did, and whether or not there was snoring, the monster did not visit the princess when Delia was there.

That night it was Greg's snores, his breathy whistles and the tinkling springs of his bed, that rocked Magdalen to wholesome sleep.

No sound came from his room when she woke the next morning but further along the passage there was the lift and dip of voices and the click of china. 'The wife cooks breakfast when she comes off shift,' Mr Hewitt had told them. 'She likes doing that. Gives her a good start to the day. Will half-past eight suit you?'

She could doze for another hour before she need get up but the paragraphs she had thought before going to sleep returned to her and she said to herself: I made a resolution. I promised myself I would put it all down. I must prove I can do it. It makes me feel as if every muscle is stretching to split and every bone is about to crack open. It's worse than holding it all in. But now that I've started, I mustn't chicken out.

Therefore she fetched the notebook, propped herself against the headboard and, as exactly as she could remember, she scribbled down what she had thought out the previous night. Then she continued:

At her first school, the princess was happy. Each year she was put in a higher class and she always sat next to Delia who remained her best friend. Whenever Delia played with the princess and slept in her chamber she kept the monster away. But it came about that the princess asked Delia to stay less and less often. The reason was she grew afraid that one day the monster would become angry that she preferred to have Delia with her; he would not be deterred; he would come when Delia was there. And, to show how cross she had made him, when he had finished he would go to Delia's bed. She did not explain to Delia why she was invited less frequently but she was sure that Delia understood. Because her friend had a secret as well. The princess knew that Delia had a monster, too. Everyone had. Delia's father did not employ a gardener but that made no difference. Gardeners did not send monsters.

In the beginning the princess had tried very hard to believe that the monster was sent by the gardener. She had argued to herself: It cannot be the king my father who comes. He would not do anything he knew I did not like. It must be the gardener's monster, and he is pretending to be king. But, since the gardener had threatened her, she had grown a little older. At school her friends did not believe in magic although they liked it in books, and gradually the princess had to admit she had been wrong. 'Monsters are not sent by gardener-wizards,' she said to herself. 'They come when they wish. Father-monsters don't need gardeners to let them out; they are not magicked into being monsters.' She could not deceive herself any longer. 'Even a king can become one,' she concluded, forlorn.

So, many months before she and Delia started another, bigger school, the princess had stopped asking her friend to come to stay in the castle. She did not think it was fair that Delia should be visited by the king-monster as well as the one in her own house. She told Delia that she had to help her father with tasks in the castle and she spent the time playing alone.

Then one day something extraordinary occurred. It was during the first year at her new school.

Each morning the king would check that her uniform was tidy and that her books were neat in her satchel and he would wave goodbye to her at the school gates. However, sometimes he had to travel to the furthermost corner of his kingdom. Then, the lady-in-waiting would stay the nights in the castle, but on this occasion Joanna had left and a new lady-in-waiting had not yet been engaged. Therefore the king appealed to his ready helpers to give lodging to his daughter while he was away. Delia had an infection and the princess stayed with another friend. She was called Gail.

The house where Gail lived was not built of stone like the castle; its walls were made of bricks held together by mortar which was crumbling and cracked. There was no wide curving drive, only a path which began at two posts without a gate between them, and no portcullis threatened above the front steps. Most of the day the door stood open and people walked in and out freely. Gail's house had no baize-covered door that led down to the dungeons, or long passages or dark closets and niches; above the three bedrooms there were no other floors or a turret where you could keep toys or hide. Hiding was not possible in Gail's house. But it was not necessary, as the princess was to find out.

At the back of the house there was a garden, at least, that was what it was called, but it was unlike any garden the princess had seen. Gail's lawn was not smooth and green like those at the castle; neither was it left uncut and white with daisies as was Delia's. It had never had a chance to grow for it was a play park in miniature. There was a swing and a slide and a climbing frame and a tricycle and a cart for Gail's brother Kevin, and cricket stumps and a football net for Peter, and a netball post for Gail, and a play-pen for the baby. Nor were they the only people who used all these things. Children came from far and wide and their shouts and their laughing and their arguments made such a noise that it penetrated the walls and windows and echoed through the whole house. This would continue until these friends and their sisters and brothers had gone home to supper, and Gail's mother would say as she waved farewell to the last, 'Now for some peace and a quiet house.' By which she meant quieter, for it was never truly quiet. There was always some noise. The baby wailed and grumbled; the cistern and water-taps clanged; conversations were shouted; records were played at maximum volume; orders to reduce it were yelled; boys' feet pounded or skidded; chairs were never lifted to the table but dragged across the tiled floor with an ear-bruising scrape. In that house the princess never listened to the silence with only her heartbeats for company. Neither did she avoid other sounds that might give her away: she did not practise with any lock until it could be turned without clicking; she did not jump from rug to rug in the hall so that her shoes should not make a tap; she did not tiptoe up to Gail's room hoping she was not observed, and she did not lie in bed wondering whether she might have an unbroken sleep. Not after she had spent several nights there. She knew that she would. Because she had learnt something else.

Each night when the family had settled, the father would go into the boys' room and the princess would hear him say: 'Right you are, chaps! The day's over. Inside the bed not on top of it, Kevin, and that lorry off the floor. Peter, pyjamas on, walkman off and in thirty seconds, so is the light. Good boy, Kev. Happy dreams. And you, Peter.' Then he would make the one pace to Gail's door, knock and say, 'You girls settled down? Let's hope the baby sleeps through. Good-night, then.' That was all.

Soon the two would fall asleep and the princess was not disturbed by steps padding outside their door. When she woke in the mornings it seemed that Gail's father-monster had not come. At first she reasoned that just as Delia had caused her king-monster to keep away, so Gail's monster had not come because the princess was there; but she was puzzled. There was something about Gail and her father that was different from herself and the king. They talked and joked and disagreed and criticised and ignored each other, but they didn't *watch*. The princess asked herself: Can it be that Gail is not visited by a monster? The question was disturbing and she was not sure that she wanted an answer. She sensed that it might upset everything she had grown to believe.

She assumed that all fathers changed themselves into monsters. It was part of their being fathers. She was certain of that because it was through your father that you learnt what all other people did. You washed your hands before eating; you were polite; you did not interrupt; you were thoughtful and considerate; you finished your homework so that you, too, would be clever and admired some day out there in the big world. You did not question any of these ways of behaving or thinking because they were the right things to do, so you did not refuse when the monster-father asked you to do things you did not like. What he did was customary. All fathers did it, and you carried out what they commanded, no matter what it was.

However, in Gail's house the princess suspected that this did not happen. And finally, one night after the father had knocked on the door and whispered, 'You two there: happy dreams!' she took a deep breath and asked, 'Is that all?' 'All what?' was Gail's answer. The princess hesitated. She did not know how to go on. So she repeated, 'Is that all? Doesn't your father do anything else?' 'Like what?' 'I don't know. Like anything. Like coming in,' she was stammering, 'for a chat.' Gail was astounded. 'What? Now? You're joking! He's had enough of us by this time of night. Why? Does yours?' Already the princess was beginning to feel a new kind of misery

creep through her. Bleakly she answered, 'Sometimes.' 'The only time Dad's set foot in this room was
to tell me off for pulling that clothes-rail down. Oh,
I didn't think! It must be different when there's only
you and your dad. Are you homesick? Do you miss
him? I wasn't thinking, honestly I wasn't. But don't
fret. He'll be back soon.'

As she said this, Gail put a motherly arm round her
shoulders and for a few moments the princess rested
against her friend's chest. The comfort was given for
the wrong reason but that was not why she finally
drew away. Her assumption had been mistaken.
She knew now why her king-monster called her
Special. It meant that what was done happened only
to her. Neither Delia nor Gail nor anyone was visited
by a monster. And although the princess continued
to play with them she did not permit any more
hugging. Because she was different; she did not fit
in.

Magdalen stopped and wiped the haft of her pen. The
sweat disgusted her; it seemed viscid and thick as glue, but
more hampering was the constriction in her throat, the
sensation that she would choke. It was a relief to see that
she had no time to write any more. She returned the notebook to her bag, collected a towel, found the bathroom
and took a shower. Then she strolled out to the garden
where Greg was kneeling to examine a plant.

'You don't look at all bad today,' he greeted her. 'I was
hoping you'd come out because we need to have a word

about money. I haven't enough cash to pay Mr Hewitt. Have you any?'

'I've got twenty-one pounds seventy p.'

'Blimey! Sure you wouldn't like to round it up or down?'

'It's what I kept after putting last week's wages in the bank.'

'Saving up for something?'

'For Edinburgh. I have to stash away as much as I can.'

'I've got a loan.'

'I'll apply for one. Dad'll want to give me a regular allowance but I shan't take it. I'll never accept his money.'

Greg remembered standing at the door of the repair shed, seeing her forcing the tube over the exhaust pipe of a car. Later she had screeched, panic-stricken, refusing to be taken home; and there had been the desperate, 'No. Please!' when Melanie had asked if she wished to speak to her father. The man must be some sort of bully, he thought; probably violent. 'It'll be wisest to have a clean break,' he remarked.

She thought: A clean break, yes. But can he imagine what from?

As they went into the bungalow for breakfast Magdalen paused, looked at the unchecked garden, and felt the anger bud stir and shoot up.

With his mouth full of cornflakes, Greg asked, 'Did your . . . did anyone ever go on at you when you were a kid about one hour in bed before midnight being worth two after?'

'No.'

He persisted despite her lack of interest. He disliked her being preoccupied; he did not wish her to dwell on what she had done in the petrol station or the reasons for it. 'My parents used to say that, when I was trying the usual tricks to delay going to bed. It was the only argument they could think up.'

'There was no argument in our house. There were rules. I'm afraid I kept to them.'

He raised an eyebrow but did not comment. 'Well, you know, this morning for the first time in my life I thought that perhaps the old folks had got a point. Last night I must've been in bed before ten, so by midnight I had clocked up the equivalent of four hours by their reckoning, and the seven hours after that brought the grand total to eleven. I felt great. I don't think I've been up at that time since I was dragged screaming from my bed with Howkins Croup.'

She laughed. 'You must have been a clever kid, screaming when you had croup.'

'I'd forgotten I was speaking to a medic-to-be. OK. I'll settle for measles. Anyway, I can tell you that when I got up, the day was as new. At least it was here in Northumberland. No one had had a go at the air; I could taste the oxygen in it; the birds were carolling; the sheep were nibbling; the grass was sprouting and the half pint of tea that Mr Hewitt drew had a head on it like the best Murphy stout.

'That was delicious,' he complimented Mrs Hewitt as she removed their cereal bowls, 'and I'd like the whole fry-up, please, with an extra slice of bacon and another egg if you can manage them.

'That's not all,' he continued as they waited, 'you have time to fit in a few jobs. I telephoned Melanie.'

'You didn't! Not before breakfast!'

'I forgot that. Mainly because I'd forgotten something else. Her PIN number. Here it is.' He showed Magdalen his hand. On the back was written in ball-point pen: 1789.

'Did you call her out of bed?'

'Something like that. I hadn't intended to and I got the impression that the call wasn't well timed – there was a lot of loud interruption from her man – but Melanie was pleased I rang. She had news. Your father had been on to her again. Not a man to leave a stone unturned.'

'He can shift mountains.'

'Well, he didn't shift Melanie. His line was that he was desperately worried about you; he knew you were under some stress. He didn't specify what that might be but he thought that you might get in touch with Melanie since she was one of your teachers and he asked her to contact him immediately if you did. She said that she couldn't undertake to do that. It came as a real surprise to him.'

'When my father makes a request, it's an order.'

'Melanie got the message but she didn't budge. She told him that if a pupil of hers – and you aren't that any longer – confided anything, she wouldn't dream of passing it on without the person's consent. He really admired her for that; people with such integrity were thin on the ground nowadays – Melanie said the flattery was sickening – and he was appalled that somehow he had been misconstrued. He didn't ask her to betray confidences. All he hoped for was that, should his daughter get in touch with her,

Melanie would let him know. He hesitated to say this, but in these circumstances he believed that a father had such a right. Melanie told him that she thought it unlikely that you would ring her but, if you did, she would explain that he was worried and leave the rest to you.'

'It was good of her to hold out.'

'Why should she *not*?'

She was puzzled by his question. 'I suppose because she doesn't have to, does she? I'm sorry he's getting at her. He knew something was going on the other evening. So he's decided Melanie's implicated.'

'Well?'

'I didn't intend her to be.'

'But she is, and she'll fight your corner.'

'No one else would. Even if they imagined I was in one.' She smiled; the knowledge she had this champion was invigorating.

So Greg chose not to recount another telephone conversation Melanie had described. He did not think Magdalen should learn that the headmaster, as well as her father, had attempted to coerce Melanie into revealing what she knew. It would renew Magdalen's disquiet at having placed Melanie in a difficult position and at the moment she looked relaxed and happy as she tackled her bacon and egg.

Ten

'Melanie, I don't like to impose school matters upon you during the holiday,' Harley Gresham had begun, 'but we've been asked for assistance. Can you spare me a minute?'

'Of course.'

'I've just received a visit from Mr Lindsay Wilde, Magdalen's father. You will have heard that she's run off again.'

'Mr Wilde rang me earlier this evening.'

'So I understand. He seemed to feel that you would know something about it.'

'I can't imagine why he should.'

'I didn't ask him to elucidate. What concerned me more was another impression you appear to have given him. Apparently, if I understand him correctly, you showed a reluctance to divulge the girl's whereabouts, should you be told.'

'I said it was Magdalen's choice. Has Mr Wilde any idea why she has gone – again?'

'He believes it must be related to stress of examinations.'

'She took those two months ago.'

'The reaction can be delayed.'

'But surely not when she's just heard her results? And has a place in the university which is her first choice? I'm surprised her father hasn't anything to say about that.'

Harley Gresham feared that he had lost the initiative in this conversation. He was beginning to wonder whether he had been wise to phone. Melanie Howkins could be very searching. This was a splendid attribute; it kept his pupils on their toes, but it was less praiseworthy when employed in discussions with senior members of staff. Namely, himself. He must pull this conversation into line again, make his point and ring off.

'We have no way of knowing the girl's motives at the moment, Melanie. What is more pressing is that Mr Wilde is anxious to get in touch with her. He is distraught. He thought he had weathered all that silly business of Magdalen's running away from home; as, indeed, did I. He had planned to take her up to Edinburgh this morning. Rather than place her in university accommodation, he had decided to set her up in a flat and they were going to choose one.'

'They were going to do that?' She was thinking: What's wrong with university accommodation? Why should he prefer her to be in a flat, and by herself?

'They were indeed. There is nothing the man wouldn't do for that daughter of his and the thanks he gets is, she disappears. He hoped to deal with the matter during this brief visit, but he has to return to Amsterdam tomorrow with it unsettled; it's impossible for him to be away any longer.'

'I see.' She asked herself: Am I getting the vibes right? Obviously Lindsay Wilde's worried about Magdalen, yet he's going back to Amsterdam. Presumably he expects her to turn up. Is the real issue this flat – accommodation? I'll have to think about it.

'I've undertaken to do everything I can,' the headmaster told her. 'One is to let him know where to contact Magdalen if anyone learns where she is. I take it that I can rely on you, Melanie, to pass on any information?'

'I've already said what I'm prepared to do. Magdalen is eighteen.'

'Since her education is not finished, she remains financially dependent.'

'I'm sure she'll be fully aware of that.'

'Well, my wife is signalling. It seems that supper is ready. I won't hold you up any longer. I look forward to your passing on any news, should it reach you.'

All Greg reported of that conversation was, 'Melanie says your father's returning to Amsterdam today.'

'That was his plan.'

Remembering her fear the previous morning, Greg had expected a more positive response. 'But you were afraid he would follow you.'

'I was, till we got out of the town.'

'And now you could be anywhere!' He raised his tea cup to toast their success.

'Yes. I've done this before, you know.'

'I gathered that from Melanie.' He hoped she would explain and give the reason but she said nothing more. So he asked, 'How long was it before he found you?'

'A few days, but not he himself. He hired a private dick.'

'No!' Instinctively Greg glanced over his shoulder, then blushed.

'Don't panic. There's no one lurking behind the curtains. I've gone past the age when I'll be searched for, fetched back.'

'I suppose you're right. All the same, I'm pleased I'm enjoying a hearty breakfast. Build up my strength for emergencies.' He stretched for toast, dug into the bowl of butter. 'Now about paying for this. My fifteen quid and your – what was it, twenty-one pounds seventy – will cover it, then we'll have to find a cash point. There's one in Alnwick.'

'But that's going back. Can't we stop on the way?'

'What is the way?'

'To the coast.'

Greg began to spread the toast with butter. The knife moved very slowly. She realised he was waiting. He was asking her to name the place.

'It's a small village.'

He nodded.

'Not far from a bay. It's got sands.'

'They often have.' What's the matter with her? he was thinking. Why can't she spit it out? It's as if she were being asked to give the map reference for the lost island of Atlantis.

He was still waiting. At last she muttered, 'I think it's called Embleton.'

'There won't be a cash point there,' he told her, trying

to sound as if they were finishing off an ordinary conversation. 'We're in bartering country. Mr Hewitt says that Alnwick's the nearest place with a bank.'

Magdalen thought: He's made me tell him and I didn't want to share; it's my place; it's rare and private; it would be impossible if he came.

Greg was saying to himself: Why couldn't she tell me earlier? Was it because she daren't mention the sea? Is that another way she might try to commit suicide? He remembered Melanie's remarks that morning: 'You have to reach extremity to attempt it and I wouldn't have thought a dominating father was enough, particularly when she's about to leave home. But I'm no expert. If she wants to talk, she'll need someone to listen.'

So, driving down the track from the bungalow, he remarked as casually as he could manage, 'I don't know this coast at all, Magdalen. I was thinking that while I'm here I might have a look.'

'There's plenty of it.'

'Do you intend to stay long at Embleton?'

'I've no idea. I just want some space.'

He winced. How about that for giving me the boot? he asked silently. Aloud, he told her, 'Fine. But you might like us to join up again and I could take you wherever else you wished to go. Anywhere would be new to me.'

Magdalen did not answer. She was angry with herself for not anticipating this might happen and at the same time was agitated at the prospect of failure. Everything would be spoilt, utterly destroyed if she knew he was hanging about. She would feel as if she were out on parole; she would feel his eyes looking over her shoulder. The place would have neither mystery nor remedy if she knew that, beyond the lanes and the dunes, he was there.

He said, 'Melanie's in no hurry for the car.'

She longed to see it, that stretch of damp beach; she longed to feel the touch of its sand and the brine on her skin; she longed to run again, bold and unencumbered, into the wind, her feet making prints clean and un-smudged. There you could scratch into the sand the things you could not speak.

'You could give me an idea of when I should pick you up.'

His persistence infuriated her. 'Do I have to make plans?' she demanded. 'Why don't you ask me for a complete timetable, the day, hour and minute? Like my father?'

'I was only making an offer.'

'Well, it's one I can refuse. If you really are heading for Alnwick, that was the turning.'

'Damn!' He drove until he found a place where the grass verge widened, then he reversed but paused before pulling out.

'Look, Magdalen, I'm not expecting you to have an itinerary planned in every detail. All I'm saying is, if you want to move on, I could stick around and take you there.'

'That's not what you're saying. You've decided to take on the job of permanent warder, only you'd feel better if I agreed.'

'It's not true! I'm trying to work something out that's best for you.'

'Exactly. You're doing the working out and claiming it's for my good. That's the usual way it's done.'

'How do you mean, the usual way?'

'The way I'm used to. I'm persuaded into something I don't want. It's called manipulation.'

'I'm not trying to manipulate you.'

'It sounds very like manipulation to me.'

He was being accused of the same behaviour as a tyrannical father and he hated her for making the comparison. She was sitting in the passenger seat; he could feel her close to him. Involuntarily, his hands made fists round the steering wheel.

She was saying, 'I can hear it a mile off. In fact, my hearing is so acute, I know when it's going to happen before it even starts.'

He swung into her face and began, 'Then why . . . ?' But the sound of his voice, harsh and ugly, stopped him.

'Why?' she repeated. She had not blenched at his tone; it was the word that had shocked her. 'Why? Why? Why haven't I prevented it all these years if I knew it was coming? Better still: Why haven't I prevented *him*, full stop? Good question. I'm working on it.' She frowned through the windscreen as if the hedgerows opposite might surrender the answer. Then she shrugged and murmured, 'I need time.'

They were silent. A wagon loaded with cattle food passed by them; a woman on a bicycle accompanied by a sniffing dog. Greg was embarrassed and troubled by what he had heard and his resentment faded. What did she mean when she wondered why she hadn't prevented her father, full stop? Was she giving a hint he was supposed to pick up? He could not decipher it. Looks as if I'm bang in the centre of the battle zone now, he thought, and they've got ground to air missiles and TNT while all I've got is a fowling piece and a bag of small shot.

He said gently, 'Magdalen, honestly I wasn't trying to take over. I sincerely wanted to help.'

'I suppose so,' she conceded. 'Don't worry.'

'You do understand, don't you, that it's hard for me not to interfere after yesterday.'

'That's over.'

'Is it? Truly? You don't want to go to the sea in order to . . . you know?'

'What? You didn't think . . . ? Is that it? No, I do not! I've no intention.'

'I'm glad.' He was sure that she was not lying. He put the car in gear and moved into the road. 'Next stop Alnwick, and a cash point. Then I'll take you to Embleton and clear off.'

'Ace. Thanks.'

After that, back to normality, he thought, and tried to stifle the regret. He wanted to say, 'It's been a funny twenty-four hours,' (funny?) 'and it's had its moments,' (no!) 'but there was quite a lot that wasn't at all bad.' What he heard himself saying was: 'It wasn't only because of yesterday, Magdalen, that I was wanting to stay around.' Be careful, he warned himself; you've got to get this right. 'It's because of you, yourself.'

She was flustered, unsure how to answer him. His words seemed sincere; they had no double meaning; they did not predict anything else. 'Thank you,' she said. Because that sounded so stiff, she added, 'Thanks.'

He wouldn't want to stay around if he knew the truth, she told herself. He would run off. He wouldn't be saying: It's because of you yourself. If he knew, if he found out what was hidden, he would be frantic to get rid of me. The mere thought of me would make him sick.

Magdalen stared at the road but she did not see it. In her sight was a girl packing her case in a friend's bedroom, ready to return home.

After the princess had stayed with her friend Gail, she returned to the castle desolate and cold. She had believed that everyone had a father monster that came in the night and must be obeyed. But Gail had no monster. It seemed only to herself, the princess, that one came, where thick walls muffled noises, where chambers were empty, where the drawbridge was raised and the gates chained against those who might venture to knock. And when she smelt the scents of the garden and found by her bed the layered frill of petals and heard the word, Special, the name had a new meaning. It meant that she resembled a prize rose that was clipped and jealously possessed. It meant that she was different, separate from all others. It meant that what had happened with her father was abnormal; it did not conform to the usual pattern and she was desperate to prevent anyone finding out.

Therefore, from that day forth she guarded her

secret and became even more diligent in concealing her true life with the king. She could anticipate a crisis and took pains to prevent it; before the woman arrived to sweep out the castle she removed any evidence of his visit that the king-monster had left; when she and the king were seen together, she made sure that she appeared an attentive and happy companion; her speech and manner were a constant proof that he was a king, virtuous and dearly loved.

All this was noted by the king and he expressed his satisfaction with many costly gifts. He did not suspect the true reason for his daughter's care that the truth should not be detected. He found another more suited to his vanity and pride. He interpreted her behaviour as a sign of complicity. He believed she was eager to enjoy all that they did.

Then in the night when the king-monster came to her, his voice told her that this was her desire; it said that she was to blame for it, that she had bewitched him with her beauty. Gloating, it claimed that her purpose had always been apparent and that her kisses in childhood had been her unblushing promise of what was to come. And she heard herself called names that are written in lavatories, hissed at street corners or shouted, hateful and insulting, behind locked doors. Then the monster would disappear with the darkness and at dawn there would be just the king left who would prepare breakfast for the princess his daughter, would fetch her blazer and take her to school.

But she did not change in the mornings. The night names stayed with her through the day; they were scrawled on her skin, a monster's graffiti, and she was fearful they would be seen. 'Are they conspicuous?' she asked her looking-glass. 'Can they be read?' But no words were visible. The princess thanked the glass for its discretion but she tried a further test. 'Perhaps the eyes of my schoolfellows are clever,' she suggested, 'and can see through fine silks and rich furs.' So she took off her garments and ordered, 'Now tell me what can be seen.' But again no words were uncovered. The looking-glass showed her a young woman grown sturdy and tall. The princess was relieved that the words were hidden but that did not reduce their effect. They were like live things on her skin spreading their stain and she could seek no salve to cure this disfigurement; it was her private, unutterable secret.

Some years after this, when the princess was about to enter the Sixth form, the woman who had replaced Joanna left her work at the castle and another woman came to manage it. She was called Mrs Brook and, like Joanna and the rest of the servants, she did not sleep in the castle but came in most days. She was kind, as were all the women who had worked there, and she asked the princess, 'Are you unhappy? You are very pale.' When the princess shook her head, she said no more but she was not satisfied. One day she told the princess, 'I'm worried about you. Sometimes I catch you looking so

miserable. Is it something to do with a boy-friend?'
'I've finished with him. I decided he wasn't my sort,'
the princess answered. Mrs Brook raised her eye-
brows. 'A pity,' she remarked. 'Perhaps you aren't
sleeping well?' The princess lied, 'I've never slept
better.' 'In that case, you must need a tonic, or
vitamin tablets. I'll get you some.' She then added
carefully, 'I want you to know that you can always
confide in me. Whatever it is. I've seen a bit of the
world, how it works. You'll promise me you won't
hesitate to come to me if you ever need help?' The
princess mumbled that she would, while she thought:
Does she guess? Can her eyes see the words that are
written upon me? Then Mrs Brook said, 'It is un-
fortunate that you have only your father. Sometimes
a young woman needs a mother she can talk to.'

This remark startled the princess. The thought of
the queen her mother gave her hope. 'I can show
myself to her,' she whispered. 'She loves me and her
eyes will be piteous. At the touch of her fingers the
names will vanish away.' So she went in search of the
queen's dressing-table. At last she found it in the
topmost chamber of the castle and it was covered
with dust. 'I have been neglectful,' the princess
moaned. 'It is many years since I attended to this relic
of the queen.' With a rag she swept away the
cobwebs; with polish she gave it a glow, but however
much she rubbed no countenance rose to smile at
her, no hand reached to caress. All that breathed
there was the princess's own face.

She never returned to the queen's dressing-table but before she left she removed the lipstick from the drawer and arranged the rags to protect its surface from dust. Then she wandered through the castle moaning, 'The queen will not come. She will not answer my call.'

Magdalen opened her eyes and saw they were entering a town. She heard Greg say, 'We're nearly in Alnwick. Watch out for a cash point.'

The roof of the car flattened his hair which was tawny coloured, drawn into a pony-tail. His right hand was firm on the steering wheel but his left was there only as a token and dangled by a hooked thumb. He drove competently but he knew nothing about cars. She had taught him to change a wheel.

'The queen will not answer my call,' the princess repeated. 'She is too distressed. She has perceived what my looking-glass did not dare; she has read the names which are smeared upon me and she cannot look upon them or stroke them away.' That was her sad lament. But she had learnt how to command her emotions and depend on herself, so one day she declared bravely, 'I must manage without help.'

She remembered Greg had said: I sincerely wanted to help. Because of you, yourself.

'I must manage without help,' the princess told

herself. 'Indeed, I shall have to. I have no choice.' Of that she was certain. The queen loved her daughter dearly, yet at the sight of the names written upon her, she had fled. Others, who loved her less, would not remain with her. The words must be for ever concealed.

Greg said, 'There's a bank, and a cash machine. Parking is further up, on the opposite side.' He drove into a space and turned off the engine. 'Look, Magdalen. See where I've parked? Try to remember it because I've been thinking that perhaps you might change your mind and decide you'd like another lift. So I'm prepared to be here tomorrow morning, with the car. It's up to you. No hassle if you're not interested. I know, obviously, that you're going through a rotten patch and I don't wish to pry, but if you decide you want to talk, well, I'll be here.'

'I'll remember.'

'Good. I shan't be a minute, fetch us some of the ready.'

Magdalen watched him cross the road and stroll along the pavement. She opened the passenger door, slid out and walked to the back of the car. Greg had reached the cash point. He was leaning into the wall checking the figures that he had pencilled on his hand. She remembered the hands. They were strong, powered by taut muscles in the wrists; she had been unable to prise them off. Twice they had prevented her from carrying out her intention. Now one was crooked over the keys like a piano player and the fingers tapped. They were long and bony, as were other fingers, but Greg's did not crawl and probe.

120

She could not tell what his eyes saw. It was impossible to know what he might suspect. He had said he did not wish to pry, but if you let yourself talk there was a risk that you might say more than you intended.

No one must be permitted to read the names scribbled upon the princess. They were her shame.
Her shame.

Greg was hunched over, waiting for the notes to be dispensed. His eyes were on the machine. Swiftly Magdalen turned to the car, saw that he had left the key in the ignition, pulled the driver's door open, and climbed in.

Eleven

The car was not as reliable as her father's but the engine was warm and started without the choke. She had checked that no vehicle was approaching and had backed on to the road before Greg had withdrawn the cash. Then he was running up the pavement, tacking to avoid pedestrians who halted or scuttled, startled by this man sprinting by the side of a small red hatchback, who was waving a clutch of clean notes, shouting, banging upon the echoing metal until the car drew away.

It was great to be driving a car again, Magdalen exulted as she steered through the town. Hadn't it been a marvellous achievement passing the test? Not only in itself, but the managing of it. Hadn't she been cunning? Saving up her wages from Saturday jobs, enrolling with a driving instructor ten miles away so that no one should hear of it, rushing off to lessons straight from school. Hadn't she found plenty of excuses if by chance she arrived home after him? Plus the plea of hockey then tennis. As a result, he had bought her a new racquet, a flashy job. Gail was happy to use it so by the end of term it looked plausibly used. Naturally Gail hadn't been told about the lessons, but she wouldn't have understood if she had. She would have said: Why keep them dark when your father wants you to get a licence, not realising that she had stated the reason. Didn't her father control her enough? She wanted a driving licence as much as her father wished her to have one, but this way the decision was hers.

Nor did that end her success in frustrating him. Without a licence there was no point in her having a car. 'I would love you to have one,' he'd tell her, offering it like a school prize for good conduct or satisfactory progress. 'You'll change your mind,' he'd laugh. 'I'll guarantee that in a few months you'll be clamouring for lessons.' (Clamouring for lessons! Already she'd had six!) 'By the time you leave school, you'll be keen to drive your own car.'

But she didn't want one, she had his. Thus she kept her principles and at the same time had the pleasure of driving. The joke was superb, the best all-time winner. Driving his car *without his knowledge* was even more gratifying than his not knowing that she'd passed the test.

And hadn't it been glorious this summer while he was away? Waiting until night had thickened the dusk; leaving the lamp in her room lit so that Mrs Dawson spying from the house opposite should think she was still working; avoiding the creaking gravel as she walked round the house; offering thanks that the garage stood out of sight at the back; heaving up its door already oiled; then letting the long elegant saloon roll down the slope to the road before switching on the engine, keeping it in low gear down the hill, changing into third and down again, pausing at a junction, into the town and as quickly out of it. And on to the long undulating road that lay under the crest of the moor.

She would sit back, the car holding the road as it swept round bends, skimmed past jutting walls, slowed at sudden corners, its gears responding silently to the slightest flick of a finger, its clutch and brakes ready for the softest pressure of her feet. It was a splendid car, and it seemed to her that it was eager to escape with her, to take to the road. So stabling it again in the garage, swabbing off the dust and polishing the chrome to conceal its use from Mr Hustler's eyes, she found herself talking to it as if it were sympathetic, alive. The secret it shared with her was not painful or disgusting and when its headlights cut a swathe through the darkness and its sun-roof framed the stars, it pointed her away from the cares of the present and freed her from the past.

That feeling returned to Magdalen as she drove out of Alnwick that morning. Ahead of her the road was a shaft directing her to the coast; above her the sun outshone the night stars and for a time she shook off shameful memories. She left them behind in the town. She left them where she had left a young man who had unintentionally caused them. She was alone at last, free of clutter; she didn't have to stay on guard to avoid being found out. And she had a steering wheel in her hands again and an engine turning at her touch. It didn't accelerate as did the other one, of course, neither were the brakes like clamping fists. This car was not half as expensive and magnificent as her father's and it was less predictable. Quirky. You had to learn its idiosyncrasies and consider its needs. When travelling at forty miles an hour it grew nervous and strained towards the grass verge, telling her that its wheel alignment was faulty; when its gears were changed down, particularly from fourth to third, it would be sluggish, indicating she had yet to master the necessary technique; when it passed over uneven tarmac, a faint rattle under the chassis warned her that its exhaust pipe was corroded or about to burst from its clip. Her father's car was luxurious; Melanie Howkins' hatchback demanded more work. That made it stimulating. Gently Magdalen moved into fourth gear, found the speed at which the engine cruised happily, discovered how to wind down the sticking window and laughed as the breeze groomed her hair and licked over her cheeks. It carried a faint tang of brine.

She reached the village where a truck driver had once dropped her. In the distance was the sea. Only a mile of fields, golf links and dunes separated her from the beach. Magdalen turned into a lane, parked at the club house, strode past golfers chatting on the first tee, crossed a stream and entered deep sand. Her shoes had filled with it the first time she had come and, apprehensive, it had been a while before she had dared to take them off. Now she immediately removed them. The first time, too, she had imagined she was lost; she had been alarmed by these strange hillocks that had lifted above her head. Their dry sand showed no paths but slid and shifted under her troughing steps. Now she did not falter. Over the soft barrier of dunes she heard what she sought.

And then she could see it. The dunes lowered, the sand

became stable and its blond colour deepened, still damp from the push of the tide. Through it, the stream she had crossed curved and flattened, became a shallow course which spread in thin threads to the sea. There they were sucked into the strong pull of bubbles as the waves lifted and broke into foam. Magdalen sighed, satisfied. At last she was here.

Along the edge of the beach, close to the dunes, a few people were scattered but she did not regard them. She did not glance where frail chalets balanced on the low cliff. The ruins of Dunstanburgh Castle, high on the headland, she might visit again later, but she did not look at them now. At present, none of these mattered. This was her place. Always it had consoled her.

After the dunes, the princess came to a shore which surpassed everything she had imagined. The sea was vast, stretching into the sky beyond the wide bay. The sand was a deep border, its edge patched by pebbles and rocks. Only the sound of the waves and birds disturbed the peace. For a time the princess stood there, shy and hesitant. She felt like a trespasser. Also, too small.

Her shoes were pinching; they were filled with dune sand. She took them off and felt the cold pasty grit under her feet. Then she was running, kicking through plashes, leaping, dancing, scrambling over low, fissured rocks, slipping on seaweed, paddling. Wading until she was drenched by the spray of breakers and their cold blued her legs. Quieter, the princess splashed along the sea's verge where the waves dropped a lace of seaweed and worm-casts lay in soft whorls. She picked her way over pebbles, pink and indigo. She explored the pools between the black ribs of rock. And as she did so, in her mind sang the words: I have escaped the monster; he cannot come here.

Because here the monster was alien. He would flee from the avenging breakers which raced, furled their foam and slapped on to the shore; his skin would bloat and effervesce at the whip of the sea's salt. In this spacious world the monster's stature would shrink and he would be no bigger than a gnat, of no significance.

So, when she saw herself reflected in the stretches of water which sheened the beach, she did not see his face leering over her shoulder; when she walked on the yielding sand no prints followed her tracks; when she played among the rocks it was the tendrils of seaweed, not the slime of the monster, that stuck to her skin; when she walked to the headland and examined the high castle, what she saw was not a solid fortification but a ruined husk where no monster could lodge, and below it the cliff did not echo with his voice but with the cries of cormorants and gulls.

And the princess said: Here I can shout out the words that the monster has put on me; the wind will blow them away. So she stood on the sea's edge and tried. But the breath she drew choked her, it blocked her throat and her tongue would not work. For the monster had spread his thick potion upon it and filled her mouth. Therefore she could not say the names he gave her or describe what he did. All that was heard was the crash of the breakers and the sea-birds' mew.

The princess was discouraged. Will I ever be rid of them? she mourned. Then the sun and the waves and the light shining up from the wet beach revived her. She watched the sea froth between her toes and slide back and she declared: 'Since I cannot shout them I will say them in pictures and the sea will spread over them and wash them away.'

So she found a strong stick that had been brought by the tide and she scored a large circle in the sand. Inside it she drew pictures of the monster and of herself with him, and all the shapes that they made. When she drew their faces, hers had no features; it was empty except for a mouth. This she filled with seaweed and slivers of broken shells. Lastly along the perimeter of the circle she wrote the names that he had painted on to her flesh. When this was finished, the princess sat by her pictures and waited. The tide crept forward, retreated then returned. She watched the words fill with water and the figures lose their hideous shapes until they were indistinguishable from the surrounding sand. And as the seaweed and shells floated away, the salt water replaced them, purging the mouth.

Seeing this, the princess was clean again as she was before the monster began his night visits. Ever afterwards, when she could no longer bear his stains and the itch of his words, she would fly from him and perform this ceremony of cleansing by this sea and sand.

Thus for a time the magic of the monster was defeated and the princess was glad. But there was one thing missing; she had no one to share her delight.

'I will call the queen,' she said to herself. 'Perhaps she will come now that I no longer bear the words that the king-monster scrawled.' So she crouched by a rock pool and looked into the still water. The crinkled sand on its bed did not stir; no shape rose to smile at her, no arms stretched up to embrace. But out of this quiet water, through the reflected clouds, came a whisper and the princess heard: 'I know what you long for. I will send you a friend.'

At these words the princess raised her eyes and there, sprinkled with spin drift, his feet sparkling in the waves' spume, she saw a stranger. At first, she was filled with consternation because she feared that he had read her pictures and understood what they told. Ashamed, she rose and would have thrown herself under the high breakers but the stranger was strong and would not let her pass. His hands held her firmly but did not bruise her and, leading her on to sand that was damp and smooth, he placed his fingers round hers and guided the nib of her stick. Nervous and unsure, she followed his direction and drew as he taught but gradually there was neither pupil nor teacher. The pictures in the sand were made by silent agreement, fashioned by them both. For many hours they drew together, hand on hand, and when the tide was at its lowest ebb and the sun was setting, they paused and admired what they had done. From the rocks in the bay as far as the cliff of the castle the shore was covered with their drawn figures. Not one was distorted; not one was shrieking with hurt or cringing with disgust; not one's mouth was crammed. These figures were handsome, graceful and affectionate. Though they were carried away by the tide they did not perish. Along the bright shore their ghosts strolled, vigorous, eager for future joys.

Magdalen stretched, found that a ribbon of seaweed was looped round her feet, saw that the sea swirled round her, knocking against the shelf of rock. She rolled up her denims and gasped at the cold as she tested the depth of the water. It was a relief that it came no higher than her calves. 'I've been here hours,' she said aloud. 'Pity I can't stay.'

The princess wished to remain on that shore for ever but that was not granted. The king sent a vassal to fetch her away and her friend could not accompany her. He had come at the queen's bidding and belonged to that place. He could draw with the princess only if she had the courage to unbolt the castle gate. But he did not forsake her; he lived in her memory. True to his promise, which he had made without words, he was waiting for her whenever she returned.

Magdalen circled the rock and, wading laboriously, urgent to keep ahead of the breakers, she made for the beach. At its edge was a figure. It was profiled by the dunes behind it and she could not see its face.

True to his promise, he was waiting for her whenever she returned.

But perhaps his patience was not inexhaustible; she did not know how long he had been there. She must hurry but the water was solid; she had to cut through it and the sea bed was ridged and studded with pebbles that tripped her feet. All the time she kept her eyes on him, willing him to stay, anxious because he neither advanced to meet her nor waved. Until as she finally reached him, he held out a hand.

The hand did not grasp hers in greeting; it was cupped, ready to receive something from her, and for the first time he spoke.

'I'd like the car keys,' the man said.

Twelve

'Did you hear me?' he asked.

In spite of the sun hard on her back, she shivered.

'Well?' His hand was still held out.

The man who was demanding was made of muscle and bone; his veins carried blood; it had flushed his cheeks. 'The keys,' he repeated.

Did this person resemble the other one, the one that had drawn with her in the sand? A memory scurried then settled. 'If you're looking for a castle to sketch, there's a ruin at the end of the bay,' she told him.

He frowned, did not turn his head. 'At the moment, I just want the car.'

'It's parked by the golf club.'

'I'll find it.'

His control frightened her. She could feel his anger compressed like a fist. Fumbling, she searched in a pocket, found the keys. His fingers closed over them.

'Is it still driveable?'

Instinctively she knew that, unlike the sand man, this man would not permit the words to remain silent. He would insist they were spoken aloud.

'Is it still in one piece?'

'Of course. I can drive. I've got a licence.'

The man nodded. 'Regard these as a loan from Melanie,' he said and proffered three notes.

Melanie, she thought, and then: This is her cousin. 'I don't want a loan,' she told him. 'Aren't you interested in what I've just said?'

He did not answer. Not caring to grab one of her hands and force the notes into it, he placed them on the sand, selected a large pebble and used it as a weight.

'I had driving lessons without my father knowing. All this summer I've taken his car out at night while he's been away.'

'Really. I'm going now.' His farewell was a nod and a jangling of keys.

Bitterly she called to him. 'I suppose you couldn't bring yourself to murmur congratulations?'

He paused. 'Congratulations?'

'Yeah. It was an *achievement*. Can't you get it? Because he didn't know.'

'So what? You kept the joy-riding in the family.'

'Family? *Family?* Are you practising a joke?' Her fear of his anger had vanished. 'You're rejecting what I did, making it worthless, putting me down. One of my father's more efficient tactics. You remind me of him.'

'You've said that before.' Greg had swung round to face her. 'If it means we have to put up with the same sort of treatment, I'm sorry for him.' He didn't care what he was saying to her. Melanie's suspicions, her cautions, his own sympathy, had all been smothered by an insatiable fury during the last searching hours. He repeated, 'I'm sorry for the old chap, I really am.'

'Send him a letter of condolence, then. It'd come as no surprise. He's the tops at public relations. Cons everyone he's perfect. Any day now he'll appear in the birthday honours list.'

'You'd improve with a spot of public relations yourself. Like having a shot at an apology.'

'I've spent years being made to feel guilty. I'm pig sick of being put in the wrong.'

'But you are. Admit it. You took Melanie's car. Not *my* car. Or, for that matter, your father's. You took a car that was *lent* to *me*.' At last he allowed his anger to rip out and he told himself that he was shouting because she had behaved inexcusably. He did not admit that he was insulted at being discarded. 'Didn't it occur to you that I'm responsible for it? Didn't you think you owed Melanie some consideration?'

'I haven't damaged it.'

'And that puts you in the clear? Not doing any material damage. It doesn't matter about me. It's OK to drive off and leave me on the pavement.'

She had left him there because he might guess the names; she had left him because he had said she might wish to talk; she had left because she might weaken and tell him; because of him himself, and that was impossible; she had left because she wanted to be alone.

'I wanted to be by myself,' she told him.

'That was agreed. I'd promised to clear off. I'd also offered to be in Alnwick tomorrow if you wanted to meet me. But I suppose you'd call that manipulation,' he sneered.

'I had to get away,' she repeated.

'I'd already got that message! Why couldn't you tell me you had a licence and were able to drive? I won't say, could *ask* to drive the car. That'd mean you admitted that someone else owned it. Instead, you sneak off. As it happens, you'd finally condescended to tell me where I was supposed to be taking you, so I knew where to look. I was frantic. I was hitching lifts, walking, expecting that at every bend I'd see you piled up.'

'I can't be responsible for your inflamed imagination.'

'Hell! You've no thought of anyone else, have you? You never for one moment give a tinker's cuss for anyone except yourself. You're too wrapped up in yourself to notice other people. It's about time you came out of the hole you're hiding in and had a look round. You might be in for some surprises. You might even see there are other people in the world besides you.'

She knotted her hands behind her back; otherwise she would scratch his face. 'If I'm in a hole it's not of my making. And when I take a look round, the person I notice most is the one I don't wish to see. But you don't know what you're talking about. You haven't the first idea.'

'I have enough of an idea to see that you don't give a damn how you get what you want. If you want to nick a car, you do. The fact that it might leave another person in the shit is utterly unimportant. It's not a problem. It doesn't exist. Because you're the only one that has feelings. It's my look-out if I feel a fool. And if I'm worried crazy you'll have a crash, so what? Up to me; no concern of yours.'

'I may not be the only one that has feelings but I can tell you for sure they aren't so petty as yours. The way you're going on, your bit of trouble this morning qualifies for a complaint to Amnesty or the RSPCA.'

'So that's all it was. A bit of trouble.'

'I don't expect it will leave permanent scars. It was soon over. You've got the keys.'

His hand flexed over them ready to slash, and she was not discountenanced. She rejoiced in his fury. 'I didn't ask you to come!' she screamed at him. 'I didn't ask you to bring me up here. I was going to hitch. Remember? But you insisted.'

'Heaven knows why.' His nostrils flared. His shoulders tensed but he did not move.

She wished that his fury would envelop her, steel hard, so that she could fling herself against it, punch it until her knuckles were battered, broken, oozing blood. 'I can tell you why!' she shrieked. 'I can tell you why you stayed with me after you'd found me at the garage. You were curious, that's why. It wasn't anything to do with helping or support or the other good Samaritan reasons you dreamed up.' The words were wild. She was deaf to justice and truth. 'You brought me and stuck around because you want to know what goes on between me and my father. It's obscene. You're after vicarious thrills.'

He stared at her, his face white. She braced herself for a blow but it did not come. Instead, low on slicing breath, he hissed, 'You bitch!'

'That's one of his names for me,' and she had leapt at him, was pummelling his chest, fisting his throat, reaching for nose and eyes. 'And see, I knew! I knew you'd shudder at the sound of it.' For a moment she was triumphant, justified. 'It revolts you, doesn't it? So get your head down and wash out your mouth.' She tried to throw him, to push his head into the flowing sea. 'Salt's a good disinfectant; it'll make your mouth nice and clean. I've tried it. The only trouble is, it doesn't last. It doesn't stop your mouth from getting mucky again. It can't prevent it being filled up again with slime.'

'Stop this!' he shouted. She felt a cheek sting but she did not let go of him. One of her hands screwed the fabric at his neck, the other tore at his hair while he beat on her arms, chopped and prised at her fingers.

'Stop this!' he shouted again, flinging her off-balance as he swung a shoulder round and butted her chest, but her hand in his hair did not loosen and the other slid on to his throat and clawed. Round them the foam swelled and shrank, the sand sucked at their feet. They fought through the fringe of the sea, rock stubbing their toes, their ankles fettered with weed, her hands grabbing, his thigh protecting his groin from the thrust of her knees.

Until, wrenching his head from her grip and punching her hand from his throat, he pushed her away. His arms outstretched to hold her off, and tripping over pebbles, he told her, 'I'm going. Like you want.'

'That's it. Walk away. Else you'll get contaminated.'

'For heaven's sake! What are you talking about?'

She had tried to tell him and he had paid no attention. She had broken her silence and nothing had come of it. But now she could not call it back.

138

'Why didn't you listen?' she screeched.

'I heard you. I heard you say I'm after thrills.'

'The word you said.'

'You deserved it.'

'Yes. That's one of the things he calls me. So that's what I must be.' Her voice had gone quiet and her body sagged.

Seeing this change in her, he hesitated and his anger lessened. 'What?' he demanded.

She was whispering, kneeling in the water, and he bent down to hear what she said. 'That's what I am. He made me all those things. I'm an outcast. A pariah. Dirt. But I tried to get rid of it. I did, truly. I tried to drain it away. Look.'

He watched as she rolled up a sleeve. 'See. I tried to let it out, years ago, all the badness. But it didn't work.'

She held out her arm to him and he saw the white threads of scars. He took her wrist and knelt beside her but she knew that still he did not comprehend. Behind them the sea rose and curled and the damp on her cheek she took as its spray.

Then at last the vileness in her mouth vanished, freeing her tongue. She heard his breath catch and felt his fingers tighten on her wrist as she told him.

'I am my father's whore.'

Thirteen

Greg's expression was incredulous, his eyes scurrying over her face, but his fingers did not loosen on her wrist. For a moment she tried to release it; she wanted to crawl across the sand and bury herself under the dunes. She wanted to stop her ears to the sound of the name that her father had given her. Then the sea lifted them, a breaker climbed and scrolled, and they floundered in the gushing water, its cold frost-sharp, whistling their breath. On the wave's ebb he rose, murmured something that was lost in the crash of the breakers, and drew her up. They waded until the strength of the water diminished, the foam ran before their feet and his brimming shoes scuffed the drenched sand. And still his fingers remained on her wrist.

They stood shaking, their bodies rattled by the sea's frost. 'Need to dry,' his tongue clapped for him. 'Soaked,' and he led her through the swelling runnels and over chill pebbles. Seeing her caution as she stepped on the barnacled rocks, he asked, 'Trainers?'

She nodded across the beach to a gap in the dunes and the lifebelt hooked on its post. 'There.'

When they reached the car, he fumbled the key into the lock of the boot, lifted out their rucksack. 'Must find dry things.' Numb fingers clashed as together they wrestled with buckles, rummaged through fabric, found pants, a towel, T-shirt, a knitted jacket.

'You have them,' she offered.

'No.' He was stopped by a spasm of shivers, resisting the sun's heat. 'My anorak's in the car. Change in the golf club. If they'll let you in.'

So Magdalen found herself in the ladies' powder room surrounded by swags of lace curtains, boxes of tissues and wicker stools cushioned in chintz. Her clothes were sodden, her hair was spiked with damp, sand striped her arms and the grit of the car park pricked into the soles of her feet. Cold to the bone, she was taken by shudders but for a time she was not aware of them. She was stunned by what she had done.

She had told her secret. She had let it out. Dizzy, alarmed that she might faint, she bent over a hand basin, filled her palms with water, raised it splashing as she trembled, to her mouth. She had said it. Her throat had not been blocked; she had not choked, breathless, upon the name. The thing her father had made her. She had not hidden behind a fairy-tale princess or sought a temporary relief by drawing in the sand. Aloud, she had said it. She did not know whether all these years she had been wrong to keep silent. She did not know whether this telling was a victory, whether it could be called a success. Somehow she had torn off a gag and she sensed that with it had gone the deceit and fear that had bound her to her father. But she was too cold to feel elated; it was too soon. In the mirror above the hand basin her face looked hollow; the cheeks worked and the eyelids flickered. She felt as if she had cast off a burden, yet the muscles still ached.

Gradually she stripped, rubbed herself with the towel and squatted under the hand drier. As her body thawed in its warmth, she went through the day, the morning flight, the afternoon hours on the beach, the fight with Greg, until again she reached the way it had ended. 'Why did I say it to *him*?' she asked. At times she had allowed herself to imagine someone discovering her secret; it would happen in a detached fashion painlessly and afterwards everything would be sorted out; her father would disappear and she would get on with her life. There was never any guilt, shame, troublesome details. But now she had disclosed her secret herself. To *Greg*. She repeated, 'Why did I say it to *him*?'

Because she found him attractive and she enjoyed his company. Sometimes there was a hint of empathy between them when thoughts of her father did not intrude. Now he would think her repulsive. She had known that she must never say her father's word to him and the expression on his face had proved she was right.

She pulled on the pants and T-shirt, buttoned up Melanie's jacket and wrung out her underwear, the shirt and jeans. She was glad he would be warm in the car and by late evening he would be home. She would find somewhere in the dunes to sleep and by tomorrow her clothes would be dry. But as she came out of the powder room she was met by a steward.

She expected him to demand why she was using a private club and she measured the distance to the door.

However, the man merely asked, 'Feeling warmer? I saw the two of you come and I've put your boy-friend's togs in the drier.' He held out his hand for Magdalen's. 'There's a pot of tea for you in the lounge while you wait.' She had no choice but to do as he suggested.

She walked towards the door he indicated. Through the glass she could see Greg. He was hunched in a chair upholstered in shining dralon and behind him were matching curtains with a tasselled fringe. She had not intended to join him but he looked solitary, out of place, and that was something she understood. At the sound of the door opening he looked up and watched her as she approached; his expression was sombre. It seemed a long time before she reached him and she was aware of her long naked legs and the hem of the jacket swaying up, revealing her thighs.

'The steward's taken my jeans,' she told him. 'I can't go till he brings them back.'

In front of him, on a low table, was a tray holding milk, a teapot and two cups. Both were empty. He had been waiting. She remembered:

> True to his promise, which he made without words, her friend was waiting for the princess whenever she returned.

But that was in her fairy story. No man in real life would remain long with her after he had been told what she was.

Greg poured out tea and handed her a cup. As he drank, he looked out of the window. Golfers were emerging from the locker room; a four was strolling towards the first tee. Attempting small talk, Greg remarked, 'Lovely evening for a round;' and she answered, 'I bet they lose a lot of balls in the dunes.'

Then they were silent. Eventually she asked, 'Will you be going back tonight?'

She's proposing we separate again, Greg told himself; go our own ways. Accepting her decision, he nodded.

'You said you wanted to explore this coast.'

'Some other time.'

'It can be very cold.' She could see them in the sea, their grappling bodies lashed by the waves. 'The west coast is warmer.'

'Something to do with the Gulf Stream.'

'Yes. Swirls in from Mexico or some place.'

Afterwards, this phenomenon became one of those private jokes unbelievably silly to anyone else. One of them had only to say, 'This soup/tea/coffee's scalding,' for the other to come in quickly with 'Probably something to do with the Gulf Stream'. But that late afternoon both were deaf to what they were saying. Their minds were snared by the memory of other words.

'If you don't hang about, you should be home by ten,' she told him.

'What about you?'

'I'll find a bed and breakfast.'

He knew she hadn't enough money. She hadn't picked up the notes he had offered. He had a precise memory of them on the sand held down by a pebble; he could remember her feet kicking it away as she lunged at him

145

and the notes bobbing and skittering like dry leaves. However, he didn't protest. It wasn't important after what had happened between them on the beach.

Neither of them noticed the steward's approach. 'I thought you ought to have something to eat, after a dousing like that,' he announced. He had brought sandwiches on a platter and cakes stacked on a three-tiered stand. 'Your clothes'll be ready in another ten, fifteen minutes, according to Molly; she's in charge in the kitchen. But you're in nobody's way. It'll be an hour or two before the regulars start rolling in. No trouble,' he answered Greg's thanks and forestalled his offer of payment with: 'It's on the house. Molly's trying a new sandwich filling, so you can be guinea-pigs.'

'You're right,' he reported to Molly. 'They've had a tiff. Sitting there as miserable as sin. Can hardly bring themselves to exchange a word. They look like a pair of candidates for Relate, hand-picked.'

'This is the first food I've seen since breakfast,' Greg said.

'Yes.'

Both took a sandwich delicately, like children warned to be on their best behaviour, and tried not to gobble.

When the steward brings our clothes, what then? Greg was thinking. They would take their gear, walk out, nod goodbye — See you sometime. *Shake hands?* He cursed silently. Why, of all the women in the world, did he have to fall for her? Was he capable of driving away while she trailed in another direction without a single penny in her purse? That, it seemed, was what she wanted and perhaps

146

it was the best thing. Best for him, anyway. There ought to be a limit to what he'd put up with, make allowances for. She was in a mess but he didn't know whether he could stay around with anyone who had accused him of wanting vicarious thrills.

While Magdalen was thinking: When he goes, what shall I do? I don't care about sleeping rough, but that only brings me to tomorrow. Now that I've said it, now that I've told him, it all ought to be easy but it seems as bad as it was, only in an altered way. I've a sense that there are other things now that I'll have to face, but I don't know what. I'm not certain I can manage it by myself.

Greg watched her select a bun and remove its paper case. One of her nails was broken; it had snagged in his shirt as they fought; he had been unable to keep out of her reach; she had surprisingly long arms. The sleeves of Melanie's jacket did not come to her wrists but they covered the scars. Sickened, he tried to shut out the pictures they brought to him. Nor as yet could he think about the father. His imagination could not manage what Magdalen had disclosed. He said, 'I shouldn't have called you that, Magdalen. It was a rotten thing. I'm sorry.'

She shook her head, dismissive.

She didn't know what to say to him. She could remember him standing tense with rage, infuriating her with his control, then the one gratifying second as she watched him blench at what she had shrieked: You're after vicarious thrills. She shuddered. Was it possible to wipe that out?

'You can take the gear,' he told her and added without humour, 'Except the shaver.'

'Thanks.' He's telling me to get moving, she explained to herself. 'I have to go home some time. There's the Edinburgh thing.'

'Melanie might be able to help.'

He had not offered himself. Which was not surprising.

'Greg.' Her throat was dry. 'I ought not to have said what I did. About you.'

He could not look at her. He knew that if this went wrong he would have to walk out of this room and drive away. But it was necessary for them both that her words should not remain, rearing between them.

'If I wanted thrills I wouldn't go for them second-hand.'

'I was . . .' She was croaking. 'I was frustrated.'

'How do you mean?'

'I think . . . I think I wanted a brawl. I had to lash out.'

'It's not me that's obscene. It's him.'

'Yes.'

'I hadn't guessed.'

'Nobody does.'

That morning Melanie had said, 'To tell you the truth, Greg, I've a suspicion that the root cause is . . .' He had not heard the rest of her sentence over the noise of the pips and he had no other coins. Was this what she had suspected?

'I'm sorry,' Magdalen said. 'You've been so considerate and patient.'

'Next time you want to lash out, can we make sure you hit the right target? I don't much like being a punch-bag.'

148

She nodded. He had not said, 'can you make sure', but 'can *we* make sure'. He had forgiven her. Her terrible accusation had been laid aside. And suddenly she no longer dreaded the future, when she must guard against her father alone. She would manage it. With this other man's help. She felt the tears creeping and before she could force them back, one fell on her lap. Rubbing it away with her finger, she muttered, 'Sorry about this.'

'No need.' He wanted to say: You don't have to hide them any longer; you may cry. Instead he said, seeing the steward, 'I think our clothes are on the way.' Watching her rise, Greg felt his heart lurch.

'Well, I'm pleased to see you both looking more cheerful,' the steward remarked. 'Must be the sandwiches. Sure you've had enough? Good. Here's your clothes, nice and warm.'

'Thanks for these,' Greg said, referring to a pair of plus-fours that the steward had lent him.

'I hadn't noticed those.' Magdalen smiled. 'You look like Charlie Chaplin.'

'I wouldn't say that,' the steward intervened quickly to prevent argument. 'I'd say they suit him.'

'They're very . . .' Greg began, but looking down at them he had difficulty in finding a word.

'Roomy?' Magdalen supplied. 'Lovely evening for a round.'

'I bet you could lose a lot of balls in those dunes,' he answered.

'That's a hazard,' the steward agreed.

Then they were laughing, raucous, uncontrolled, Greg

leaning over the settle and Magdalen stooped, clutching her waist.

Greg managed to cough out, 'It's not the plus-fours. We've had a hard day.'

The steward nodded, affecting patience. 'Well, it must be improving,' he commented, 'if you can laugh.'

Fourteen

'You can't beat a pair of old breeks for comfort, my grandad would say,' Greg remarked, slapping his thighs now clad in dry denim. Without any spoken decision Magdalen was sitting in the passenger seat of the car. 'Still set on sleeping rough?'

'I didn't say I would do that.'

'No. Like you didn't mention that you hadn't picked up the three tenners.'

'I'd forgotten you might remember.'

'One thing you can rely on, if nothing else, is my memory. So what's it to be?'

'You choose.'

That's a change, he thought while he exclaimed, his head in his hands, 'Oh, no! Decisions. Decisions. I don't feel like driving far. At the moment a couple of miles is my limit, I think. Within that radius, surely there must be a pub? How about that?'

'Sounds fine.'

The one they discovered was small and had been spared the attentions of a brewery designer. Therefore the windows were not hung with folksy curtains, there was no mirror-bright varnish or fittings sprayed with gilt and the cast iron fireplace had not been repositioned under a fake chimney. Despite the season, a heap of genuine coals glowed in its hearth. Behind the beer pumps, a barmaid sat entranced by a quiz show on the television screen and pitted her wits against the contestants as she knitted.

'They won't be fetching out the dominoes till Tuesday,' she informed them, 'and it was the darts team last night.'

'I hope they didn't drink all the beer.'

She raised an eyebrow. 'You trying to be clever? What d'you think those are?' She pointed a needle at the pumps.

'I'd like an orange juice please,' Magdalen told her.

'There's none out. It's in the store. Just catch the answer to that question, will you, while I'm gone.'

They missed it, of course, much to the barmaid's disgust. 'Forgot? What were you doing, then? I hope you haven't been drinking.' She examined them warily. 'I can't do with that. I mean, you're not local.'

'I worked in a pub once,' Greg said when they were sitting at a table, 'but I didn't last long.'

'You didn't approve of customers drinking unless they were local?'

'I didn't have that particular dilemma. It was the Karaoke that finished me off. Without fail, an old chap would limp up and croon: "I'm Dreaming of a White Christmas", his wife would trill "Edelweiss", with her pals in support, someone might have a jab at "The Happy Wanderer" and there was the inevitable Elvis. So one night I tried to hot it up a bit and chose Frank Sinatra's "My Way", Sex Pistols style. Went down like a lead balloon. The landlord took me to one side and confided that it wasn't to the company's taste and I said I thought it made a change. He said the only change wanted was in personnel, particularly if it "makes a mockery", and he thought I'd be happier working somewhere else. What about you? Did you have Saturday jobs during term time?' I shouldn't have asked that, after what happened at the petrol station, he told himself.

'Yes. Dad didn't stop me. He's a great believer in extending your experience, that's how he expresses it. I didn't let on I was interested in the money, not the experience.'

'You were saving up for Edinburgh?'

'Not till this year. Before, I wanted to buy things.'

'But your father's loaded!'

'I wanted things I could choose myself. Crappy stuff, if I fancied it.'

'So what did you do?'

'Nothing very exciting. I've worked in a bookshop. That wasn't bad; you can get through a lot of books while you wait for customers. I once used to shop for an old woman every Thursday after school but she had to go into a home.' She smiled. 'I wondered whether there was any connection. I've done some baby-sitting, too. Have you ever done that?'

'No, I'd be too scared.'

'You could always take out personal insurance or borrow combat gear. As it happens, the babies were no trouble. It was the parents that got up my nose. The husband was forever asking me things like what sort of freebies my dad handed out, what advertising agencies he used, as if he was trying to pick up some tips, and the wife kept telling me it was OK to have a boy-friend in, provided I asked her first. What she was hinting was that she suspected the homework spread over her kitchen table was just a blind and that during the four hours she was away I was entertaining the local yobs, in series or groups.'

'And did you?'

'Not for the whole four hours.' However, since he did not appear to take this as a joke, she added, 'I didn't have anyone in, Greg. Least of all a bloke. One of the effects of my father.'

She said no more and he did not press her but he thought: Would it be possible to have a normal relationship with her? However it turned out, it would be a real slog. I'm not sure that it would be worth the aggro. But he knew that it would.

Lindsay Wilde did not intrude again until much later. Although his spectre persisted to circle round them, Magdalen succeeded in keeping it at bay. She wanted to enjoy chatting about ordinary things.

'Tell me about your course at the college,' she said and their talk continued, easy and without strain.

After a time he asked, 'Do you mind if I give Melanie a ring? There's a telephone in the passage behind the bar.'

'No. Why should I?'

'Because obviously I can't avoid mentioning you. But all I shall say is we're still wandering round. Nothing else, I promise. I think I should phone, though; keep in touch.'

She watched him check whether he had the appropriate

coins and stride across the room. The hair along his forehead was frizzed by the sea water; the pigtail swung. His shoulders were broad, his chest deep and muscles showed under the sleeves of his T-shirt, but he did not assert them. There was no hint that they were considered as a means to dominant power. Some day I might tell Greg about us, about my father and me, Magdalen thought.

The fairy-tale was over; it had played its part but now she felt that she must describe her secret life to someone, otherwise she would never conquer it.

Greg knows the plain fact and I've the impression he wants to stay; he hasn't cleared off yet, she encouraged herself. But perhaps he would if I told him everything; I should have to take that risk.

Might that always happen with men she was attracted to? Might every man lose interest in her if she described her life with her father?

Her breathing snagged and her eyelids twitched as the anger bud swelled.

'Mel sends her love,' Greg reported, 'and she's had an idea. About student accommodation in Edinburgh. Do you want me to tell you?'

'Please.'

'She's been rooting about and found out the procedure for applying for halls of residence and so forth. Do you know it?'

'Yes, but I haven't done anything. I thought I'd be tempting fate.'

'You daft thing! But Melanie guessed you hadn't. You have to apply by the first of next month to take up a place.'

'Yes, I remember.'

'Presumably that's what you prefer?'

'You bet!'

'It doesn't leave a lot of time so Mel's phoned the allocations office and left a message asking for the forms to be posted to you.'

'That's great. Dad wanted me in a flat.'

'Mel's told me.'

'But I calculate that I'd be safer in a university place. Dad couldn't keep turning up at a Hall or Student House. It'd look fishy.' But suddenly she was less certain. She could imagine him greeting porters and wardens, exuding charm, his arms full of roses. 'Or am I wrong?'

'You may be, but all the same I think he'd be less likely to chance it. Otherwise he wouldn't be so keen on setting you up in a flat.'

'It was the thought of that, you know . . . that made me . . . yesterday morning. I couldn't see any way out.'

'Yes; I've pieced it together, and if you could stop your father having access to you so easily, you'd have one fear off your mind.' I must be careful not to sound as if I'm organising her, he cautioned himself. 'But Mel and I think there might be a slight problem. Since asking for accommodation details, she's worried whether she's done the right thing. Your father might anticipate that you'll apply for what they call controlled accommodation, mightn't he?'

'I expect he will.'

'And he's so set on your having a flat, he'll want to prevent your living anywhere else. So might he intercept your post? Would he be capable of doing that?'

Reluctantly she answered, 'I think he would.'

'Would it be possible for him to do it? When he's away?'

'He might ask Mrs Brook to redirect my post to his office.'

'Who's Mrs Brook?'

'She's a sort of housekeeper but she doesn't live with us.'

'Blimey! Mel didn't know about her. She said that, if you decide it's necessary, she's prepared to collect the post. If you could tell her how to get in.'

'Most mornings, Mrs Brook's there for one reason or another. Except Fridays.'

'Shall you phone her tomorrow, then, let her know?'

'Melanie or Mrs Brook?'

'Probably both, but I'd start with Melanie.'

'Yes; I'll do that. You make it sound so simple.'

'Do I? I don't think the whole thing is simple.'

'No. There's a lot more.'

'Perhaps eventually you'll find ways of dealing with your father.'

She nodded but he saw that her former fear had returned so he added quickly, 'Look, don't be bothered with that now. It's getting late. We shouldn't have a miserable end to the day.'

'Especially when the rest of it has been so marvellous,' she said and they both laughed.

'Would you like chicken in a basket? With chips.'

'I could kill anything edible.'

157

'I think that's done before the chicken hits the basket. I've put it to Anita,' he nodded towards the bar which was left unattended, 'and she's agreed to venture into the kitchen. She's bored stiff with the highlights of the day's cricket. She also said they can do you bed and breakfast here if you wish.'

'And you?'

'There's another place at the end of the village, Anita tells me.'

She had also told him that she knew for a fact that there were no vacancies and: 'You'll have a job finding anywhere this time of night. It's a double upstairs, what's wrong with that?'

'Nothing at all. It's the circumstances that are wrong,' he had answered, and Anita had nodded, sympathetic.

'Like that is it, pet? Well, there are as good fish in the sea as ever came out of it. Did you say you'd have the chicken or the battered cod?'

Magdalen asked him, 'Did she know whether the other place could put you up?'

'No hassle.' He had to think rapidly; he wasn't used to lying. 'If it's full, there's a caravan to take up any surplus.'

'I've never slept in a caravan.'

'Have you not? They're smashing. Neat, no clutter, everything functional. Very comfy,' he enthused, warming to the idea of a caravan which was the nearest he'd get that night to sleeping in one. 'The top-range models have showers.' Damn it, he cursed silently. I've now got to look clean and shaved tomorrow morning, after sleeping in Melanie's car.

'You're more practical than I am, Greg.'

'Practical? Until yesterday I couldn't even change a wheel of a car.'

'That's mechanical aptitude. I'm saying, practical. Like thinking about this,' she nodded to the basket of food Anita was placing in front of her. 'Thank you, this looks lovely.'

When Anita had left them she continued, 'And arranging for tonight. It makes me feel useless.'

'You mustn't say that. It's stupid.'

'No; it makes me feel as if I've lost my grip and I'm putting on you. And Melanie. It should be me chancing my luck and you taking the room here. I'm just a nuisance.'

'You're not.' Alarmed, he asked, 'Magdalen, will you make me a promise?'

'Such as?'

'You won't do anything. Anything silly, tonight.'

'No, I won't. I promise.' Then she said, 'Greg, I feel awful about taking the room and your having to look somewhere else. I'd rather we swopped.'

'I'd rather we didn't.'

She was a long time before she said anything more, picking at her chips. 'I have to ask you something,' she managed at last. 'I'm sorry; I don't want to put you in a spot, but I have to know.' The spittle had dried on her tongue. 'Say we were on holiday together and we were . . . like . . . sharing, you know . . . a room. And say I told you what I did this afternoon. On the beach. About me and my father. Would you, would it make you decide you couldn't . . . share . . . after that?'

'To be honest with you, I can't be sure,' he replied carefully. 'I hope it wouldn't. But we're talking hypotheses, possibilities. As things are, it doesn't make any difference. Not right now.'

To Greg, his answer seemed unsatisfactory; he regretted that it sounded evasive, but he was rewarded by the relief in Magdalen's face.

Fifteen

The next morning, as Magdalen began her breakfast, Greg joined her. 'I thought we both might like some company,' he said, 'so last night I persuaded Anita to serve me breakfast here.'

'You seem to have made a hit.'

'I hope so; I'm going to ask her if I can take a shower.'

'Why's that?'

'The hot water was off at my place.'

'Was that in the caravan?'

'Caravan?' His father had once said to him, discovering a trivial deceit: Lies get out of hand, Greg; they breed like bugs. He confessed, 'As it happened, I dossed down in the car.'

'Did you? My fault.'

'No; and I was quite comfortable. Slept well.'

'I wish you'd let me.'

'I don't want to go into all that again. Let's talk about today.'

'Yes.' The previous night she had gone to bed thinking about this. She had said to herself: What will happen tomorrow? The thought of returning home gives me the shakes.

'What I've been wondering,' Greg began but was interrupted by Anita bearing food.

To his request for a shower, she answered, 'Help yourself, pet. I expect you can do with one.' She patted his shoulder. 'Circumstances being what they are.'

'Star treatment,' Magdalen commented.

'Once she's adjusted to the terrible fact that you're not a local, she's got a soft heart. She's a sweetie.'

I bet he wouldn't say that about me, Magdalen thought, aware that for a moment she was jealous of Anita. But I wouldn't be that if Dad ever called some other woman 'a sweetie'. I'd be ecstatic. I'd be up there gliding in the stratosphere if he showed an ounce of interest in anyone else. I'd be singing her praises, encouraging him, doing my best to get him married off.

Her attention returned to Greg and she asked, 'You were saying, about today?'

'I was going to ask if you'd like us to spend it together. Or perhaps you'd rather be by yourself? I've no wish to push you, even if it were possible.' He punctured the yolk of his fried egg. 'It's just that I've more or less decided to stay up here for a day or two and it seems unreasonable to have a car and for you not to use it, me cruising around and you struggling with public transport, if there is any. I can imagine that this suggestion may be about as fanciable as my stab at karaoke. But after all that went on yesterday I don't feel like just packing up and going home. Packing up! Lobbing the rucksack into the car boot. There was so much, and a lot I couldn't get my head round.' He was talking rapidly, his eyes on the food on his plate. 'Not that

I'd expect you to say more than you have already, though you're welcome to, if you wish, it's that I need some time to – I don't know – get sort of adjusted to it. Of course, I shouldn't need anyone's company to do that; I ought to be able to think it over striding along a beach by myself, but for some reason that's a rather frightening prospect. Is that odd? Anyway, you must do what you wish.'

'I'd like to come.'

'Good.' He looked up. 'Sure?'

'Yes. And Greg, I don't think it's at all odd that being alone thinking about it is a frightening prospect.' She saw a muscle in a cheek flick and said to herself: I never considered that it might be as distressing for him as it is for me.

When they had finished their breakfast, Magdalen telephoned Melanie while Greg took a shower.

'I'm glad you've rung,' Melanie said. 'How are you feeling?'

'Improved.'

'Good. Has Greg told you what I suggest?'

'Yes. I think it's great but you mustn't get involved.'

'I've already telephoned the accommodation services.'

'I know, and it was good of you to think of it. But if you go into the house to collect the post, Mrs Brook's sure to report it to my father. She's our sort of living-out housekeeper. My father would tell Mr Gresham and I expect he'd get back to you about it.' Last night she had considered Melanie's offer and reached a decision. 'I'd rather not make any more difficulties for you. So I'll phone Mrs Brook. If my father has told her to redirect my letters to him – he may not have done, but if he has – I'll . . . I'll countermand the order.'

'That's a better idea, not because I wish to avoid trouble but because the request should come from you; and for a more important reason.'

Magdalen waited. There were small noises, faint liquid sounds as if the other woman were summoning up moisture to her tongue, licking dry lips. At last she said, 'You see, Magdalen, I feel that it's necessary – crucial – that it's you that makes the stand, however hard it is, and that no one is left in any doubt that it is you who's doing it.'

'Yes, I agree. This is the start.'

'You're being very brave.'

The words rocked her. They tweaked at the waiting tears. She tried to say something dismissive like: I haven't done anything yet; and the sentence became: 'I haven't done anything to deserve your saying that.'

'We're not talking A level grades now. If you ever want any help, you will ask?'

Greg had said that he would not tell Melanie what her father was. She heard the other repeat: 'You will, won't you?'

'Yes, I will.'

'Promise?'

'I promise.' She thought: Possibly one day I shall want to tell her; and added wryly: When I've practised on Greg. 'How long do you estimate it'll be before the stuff from Edinburgh reaches our house?'

'Well, they won't hear the request I put on the answering machine till this morning, so probably another two or three days.'

'So I ought to come back the day after tomorrow.'

'That would depend on the arrangement you make with Mrs Brook. You could ask her to forward the letters.'

'We have to return your car.'

'If I need one, I can borrow Donald's.'

'Thank you.' Shouldn't she be making a confession? Saying something like: Look, Miss Howkins, I took your car without asking Greg, but it wasn't dangerous or illegal; I've got a licence.

'In any case, it's such beautiful weather at the moment I don't want to move from the garden,' Melanie said. 'I've spent the last couple of days soaking up the sun.'

It was true, the weather had been marvellous. She remembered patches of the journey, the water in a reservoir hazed by heat, hills pitched with shadow, the dust round the lorry as they fought in the car park, the sweat on her face while the sea water washed cold over her feet. Suddenly she wished she could enjoy it. 'We're using your money. Greg drew some out yesterday.'

'I'll keep an eye on it. Make sure there's some there.'

'As soon as we get back, I'll . . .'

'We'll talk about reimbursing me later. Luckily I'm not pushed this month, but if I need a top-up I'll call upon Donald.'

'Wouldn't he mind?'

She heard the other's surprise in her answer: 'Of course not. I'd do the same for him,' and Magdalen had a vision of a relationship that was unselfish, where money was not used as a weapon or a reward.'

'I'm putting everyone to so much trouble.'

'You mustn't think that, Magdalen. When it's some-thing you are willing to do, it's no trouble.'

She could not answer. Words came but she had to control the surging breath. All she could manage was a neutral: 'I'll ring again,' and to replace the handset before the breath exploded and her body was shaken by pants. When they were over, she said to herself: You're ridiculous. Reacting like that. As if nobody has ever been kind to you. There have been dozens. She thought of them: Joanna and the other women who had cared for her as a child; Mrs Brook; Delia; Gail; their parents and families; all her friends along the years. But none of them had been there when she needed them. Though you can't blame them for that, she told herself. It wasn't their fault; they didn't know. How could they, when you kept it a secret? You never even hinted, dared to make an appeal.

Greg was still upstairs in the bathroom. She could hear the water of his shower gushing down the pipe. He took a longer time than her father. Leaning against the telephone, Magdalen gazed through the open door at the end of the passage. Among the branches of apple trees globed with reddening fruit there glinted a thin stripe of the sea. I must think of this when I remember, when I remember my father in the shower and what followed, she whispered to herself. I must think of a thread of sea in those branches and the sound of water running down a pipe and myself waiting for a man to finish. Safe.

She lifted the handset, pushed coins into the slot and dialled Mrs Brook's number.

'Why, Magdalen!' the woman answered her greeting. 'How nice to hear you. Are you back home?'

'No. I'm speaking from a call box.'

'So you won't have got my card. I've left it on the hall table, to say congratulations on your results. I haven't seen you since the day before they came out.'

'Thank you.' How much had happened since then.

'You worked so hard, when your father told me you'd gone off on holiday, I said: "The girl deserves one." '

That was the explanation he had given Mrs Brook; it was a suitable one for her to pass on to the neighbours. Automatically Magdalen assumed the habitual caution. 'Did he say anything else?'

'He talked about getting you a flat where you'll be studying. Edinburgh, isn't it? He mentioned you might be receiving papers that would need attention and asked me to send them on to him.'

Melanie and Greg had been right. 'That's why I'm phoning. I expect they'll arrive mid-week.'

'Well, don't worry. I shall be going in. I'll send them off straight away.'

'This is a bit awkward, Mrs Brook, but I have to ask you to hang on to letters addressed to me.'

'Mr Wilde pointed out they could be urgent.'

A vein in her wrist bulged as she held the handset. Why did she find this so difficult? 'All the same, I'd rather you didn't redirect post to my father if it's addressed to me.'

'Since that's how you feel, Magdalen, of course I won't. I didn't like to say as much to Mr Wilde, but I thought: They're not for him, they're meant for her.

Instead of keeping them back, I could send them to you if that would suit.'

Was this a trick? Was Mrs Brook to be trusted in spite of her agreement to disobey her boss? Had that been a way of softening up his daughter so that she could find out where she was staying? 'I'm still moving around,' Magdalen told her.

'Well, if you settle anywhere, you can give me a ring,' the other answered. 'It's no bother to me either way. I know I shouldn't ask, but would the documents have anything to do with this flat your father is set on buying?'

'No; that's his business. But I do expect them to be about accommodation, halls of residence.'

'That's what you'd rather move into, is it?'

'Yes.'

'You stick to that, Magdalen. You're leaving home and you want to be living with youngsters your own age not stuck by yourself in a flat like you were in that great house, waiting for your father to turn up.'

'That's how I feel.'

'I'm pleased you do. Going to Edinburgh will be a new start.'

'Yes.'

There was a pause then Mrs Brook began hesitantly, 'I've something I want to say to you. I decided I would before you left for university and it might as well be today. You may think I've got a dirty mind and perhaps I have.' The words were coming quickly now. 'And I've told myself it's not for me to start stirring things up, all I'll do is upset her if there's nothing in it. Then I'd think: There's

168

no smoke without fire and going into that house for the past two years, I've seen some evidence of smoke. And I didn't want you going off to university believing you can't call on me for help, if what I'm thinking is true.'

Mrs Brook halted, waited for a response, but Magdalen could not speak. She had known Mrs Brook was suspicious, ever since she had said, 'You'll promise me you won't hesitate to come to me if you need help?' and, 'Sometimes a young woman needs a mother to talk to.' But that did not prepare her for this moment. Knowing that the woman suspected was not as difficult to accept as it was to hear her talk in this way.

'Well, that's that,' the voice continued. 'You can call me what you like and tell your father and he can give me the sack. It seems I've said more than I ought. I've often told myself: You have to keep an open mind, see it from all sides, she's a clever young woman and got plenty about her. It could be that she's in agreement.'

Magdalen gasped. The passage in which she stood was sucked empty of air; the floor at her feet tilted. Her throat grated as she said to the other, 'I was never in agreement.' Her answer admitted that Mrs Brook's suspicions were correct.

'Oh, Magdalen! Why didn't you tell me? I gave you the chance.'

'I know, but I couldn't.'

'You poor lamb,' Mrs Brook whispered. Then, more strongly: 'So what's to do?'

'I don't . . I haven't thought.'

'Whatever you decide, you can count on me.'

'Thank you.'

'Now you go along and enjoy that holiday,' the woman instructed, maternal. 'And start looking round for a nice young man.'

'I think I've found one.'

'Well, I never! Don't keep him waiting any longer, then. Off you go!'

'You heard, Will?' Mrs Brook enquired as she put down the telephone. 'You see, I was right.'

'All I hope is that you know what you're doing, speaking out like that. It could lead to trouble.'

'That would suit me.'

'He's a big man in his line of business, Clara. You get mixed up in it, there's no telling how it might backfire.'

'Will, that's no way to look at it.'

'I'm giving you a warning, that's all. What'll you do if she takes it to the police?'

'I'll do what's needed. Will, that man's been treating his daughter like she was his wife.'

William Brook flinched. 'It could've been no more than a cuddle now and again.'

His wife glared.

'I mean, things can get blown up. You know what young girls can be like. Romantic.'

'*Romantic?*'

'They'll romance. Think of our Sheila. She only had to see a good-looking chap walking down the road, and she'd be dreaming.'

'She wasn't dreaming of this sort of carrying on! Will, I don't want this to cause an argument between us. I don't like it any more than you, but turning a blind eye is no use.'

'I'm not turning a blind eye,' he defended. 'All I'm pointing out is, whatever story the girl has, who can say it's the truth?'

'Are you asking me that?'

William Brook recognised danger. His wife's voice had gone pinched and cold. 'I'm not questioning your sense, Clara, but we can all make mistakes.'

'Doubtless. But just let me ask you this. What would you say if you washed sheets with a particular smell on them and found rubber johnnies floating about in the loo?'

'Clara, don't. It turns me up.'

'So what do you imagine it does to Magdalen?' she persisted. 'For that matter, what do you think it does to me? It's been nagging at me ever since I suspected, but it was beyond belief. He seemed such a lovely man, a really good employer, considerate, and so careful about her. You'd have thought he wouldn't harm a hair of her head. But he didn't bring women into the house and she didn't have boys. I tried, several times I tried, Will, to get her to tell me, but she'd clam up. I should have kept at it.'

'You can't force people to say something they don't want.'

'I don't know. I should have done more to get her talking, even come straight out with it and said, "Look, Magdalen, does your father," – I don't know – "do anything you don't like?" Something on those lines. But then I'd see them out together and in spite of all the evidence, I'd not believe there could be anything wrong going on. I wish I'd taken no notice of how they behaved when they could be seen. I wish I'd managed to get her to confide in me. We might have put a stop to it months ago. But I didn't manage it, Will, and I'll never forgive myself. So now I'll stand by what I told her. She can have my word if she wants it, though I know it'll be a nasty business if it ever comes to court.'

'You never know, her leaving home and moving up to Edinburgh might settle it. If it doesn't, you'll have to find out what she has in mind. But there's one thing that's certain, Clara.' He rose, put an arm round her shoulders and kissed her cheek. 'Whatever happens, you've got my approval. I'm here. With you. You can rely on me.'

While this conversation was taking place, Magdalen was saying to Greg, 'Mrs Brook knew. I phoned her, after I'd spoken to Melanie.'

They were outside the public house, the car doors were open. They were ready to go. 'I've known she suspected. It was awful. I used to think: Does she go round imagining what Dad and I do? It made me feel dirtier. Today she called me, "you poor lamb".' Magdalen looked away from him. 'It's words like that I can't take. Melanie said, "You're being brave," then Mrs Brook calls me "poor lamb". It breaks me up. I've had to teach myself to keep tough. There could be no room for sentiment.'

He wanted to put his arms round her but he knew she would repulse them. Her precarious control would be destroyed by his touch. He watched a tear slide down her cheek then splash on the car bonnet. She took out a handkerchief and hastily dabbed. 'I'm sorry to go on like this.'

'You're not going on. Shall we make a move? This is a bit public.'

'Public?' She looked round. 'Hell! It's crawling.'

'The Northumbrian version of Piccadilly.' He stared back at their audience: a woman fiddling with the straps of a buggy, its dribbling occupant, a man revving up a tractor, two contemptuous seagulls and an incontinent dog. 'The rumour is we're a two-person travelling theatre.'

'Or a circus.'

'Let's go. You wave nicely and I'll sound the horn.'

Sixteen

After a time, Greg asked, hesitant, 'Feeling any better?'

'Yes, thanks.'

'If you still favour a beach . . .'

'I do.'

'I'll have to stop for petrol first.'

At a filling station she told him, 'While you're improving your mechanical aptitude, I'll have a go at being practical. That breakfast won't last you the day, will it?'

'It's already beginning to wear off.'

'I'll go in and buy some food; and I'll pay for the petrol, too, if you can give me some money.'

He handed her his wallet and she left him wrestling with the cap on the petrol tank.

'You're getting better,' she said when she returned to the car. 'There's practically no smell of petrol on you and only a drop or two on the wheel.'

'I'm a quick learner. Why those?' He pointed to buckets and spades that poked out of the carrier bag.

'I thought we could run to them; they were sale price, seconds. Do you mind?'

'If you want to play on the sand with a bucket and

spade, Magdalen, be my guest. I'm just worried that you've bought two of each.'

'I didn't want you to feel left out. Sometimes we'd go on holiday in Wales. Pembrokeshire. Dad used to make the most elaborate sand-castles.'

'What did you do?'

'I used to fill the bucket with sand and fetch water. I remembered that when I saw these, and I thought: Wouldn't it be nice to swap jobs?'

Swap jobs, Greg repeated to himself as he drove off the forecourt and on to the road. With me playing the skivvy, as her father never did. But he said, 'Bags I the green bucket, then. The yellow one sets my teeth on edge.'

Magdalen was digging into the carrier; she pulled something out and laid it on the shelf in front of him. 'I hope you like that. I think it's jolly, the Mickey Mouse face.'

'What next?' He reached for the watch and examined it. 'Now it's Mickey Mouse time.'

'It's rubbish, I know, but that's why I like it.' She was thinking of her father's gifts. All had been extravagant and costly; few, it seemed to her, had ever been simple tokens of love. They had been given as bribes and enticements, or to make amends. When she was a child she had delighted in them, the bows and frills and the exotic toys. But as she grew older they became loathsome and she never used the telephone installed in her bedroom; she faked an allergy to the satin sheets, hid away the lingerie and turned over the make-up to Gail.

Scrupulously, she explained, 'I bought the watch out of my own money, what was left.'

'You've already got one.'

'So have you, but you can wear this for a change.'

'It's for me?'

She nodded, shy.

Greg slowed down the car and pulled on to the grass. 'Thank you.' He didn't know what else to say.

'It's the best I could do. Though, compared with a present of a car, it's definitely down-market.'

'I'm pleased you couldn't afford a car. I'm much happier with a watch. I don't even have to wind this up. Presumably it's got a battery or something?'

She laughed, then said, 'When I saw this, I was reminded of a watch I pinched once.' Her tone was reflective.

'What did you say?'

'I think the other one was about the only thing I took that I ever actually wanted to own. It caught my eye.'

Astonished, Greg warned himself: Play this one cool. He asked her, 'What happened? Were you found out?'

'Not always, but when I was, nothing came of it. I wasn't sent away, put into care. Anything lucky like that.'

'The last thing your father would want.'

'He would arrive, after they had wheedled out of me where I lived. It was never the housekeeper who came, always him. He kept it hushed up. I don't think anyone knew.'

'I'd have to wait hours in the manager's office and there would be him and an assistant and they'd arrange the stuff on a table, like exhibits in court. They'd say, "Why is a little girl interested in these sorts of goods?" and I couldn't tell them I wasn't in the least interested. "Have you a granny?" they would ask, pointing to the elastic support stockings and boxes of corn plasters. "Is her birthday coming up?" Does anyone buy her granny corn plasters for a present? Mainly it was things like dummies and disposable nappies and feeders. Generally I did it in Boots. "I expect you were wanting these for your little brother or sister. Do you think your mummy can't afford them?" They made that deduction only on the first occasion. Once they had met my father, his car and his suit and his accent soon put them right. So when I hid under the table and he had to drag me out, screaming, all they saw was a horrid delinquent child and a long-suffering dad.'

Magdalen rolled down the window and held her face to the draught. 'It didn't end there. Dad was humiliated. I don't think I can talk about it any more.'

'You don't have to.' Greg was ashamed because suddenly it was his distress, not hers, that he wished to avoid. I'm not sure that I can take it, he said to himself. First there was the attempt at suicide and the rush here; a repressive father; lots of occasions when she'd begin to tell me something and break off; then what she said on the beach. And me all the time floundering, out of my depth, with no idea how to handle the situation. Now it's shop-lifting and we're in the land of Mickey Mouse watches and buckets and spades.

'Look, Magdalen,' he said to her, 'I told you at breakfast you don't have to talk about it. It's up to you. We can just walk, lie in the sun.'

She was looking out of the window. Beyond the fields

was the long steel cord of the sea. 'Let's find a beach. I'd like to tell you, Greg, but it's hard to describe it, and it's not the most entertaining story for you to hear.'

At last she felt she could confide. Greg knew that he should be relieved, pleased for her, but his strongest feeling was apprehension. He stretched forward. 'Don't worry,' he murmured. 'We'll manage.'

Magdalen was aware of a pressure, gentle and brief, upon her wrist.

Seventeen

In Bamburgh they found a cool space under trees to park the car and took a path that ran beside a cricket pitch and through the low dunes. The castle stretched massive along the table of rock.

'That's some pile,' Greg admired. 'It's still used, you know. Yesterday, one motorist who gave me a lift told me about the castles round here.'

He stopped and examined the walls reared above them. 'I like their bulk and their profiles against the sky. I don't think this would be the best position for drawing this one.'

She felt vulnerable, threatened by its ponderous weight. It looked as if it might crack the rock upon which it stood. Turning her head from it, she asked, 'Do you remember Gail, the one in leathers you talked to at school?'

'She'd be hard to forget.'

'Gail told me you meant to go into Leeds, to have a look at Armley Gaol because it resembles a castle.'

'It does, up to a point. It's a fake, of course. Just a prison.'

That's what castles are, she answered silently. 'You were going to do a strip cartoon? Gail said some kind of fairy-tale.'

'I haven't thought of anything yet.'

Modern, Gail had reported; up to date. 'That gave me an idea for writing down what happened.'

'That's odd, sort of sinister. Is that what you were doing in the car, the day before yesterday?'

'Yes. I'll tell you.'

There were people on the beach but, as Greg commented, they didn't have to jostle for space. The sands were so long and broad that groups could spread out. Some, having chosen their patch, corralled it with wind breaks and set up house: gas burner and ice box in the kitchen area, inflatable mattresses in the sun lounge, tanning aids and barrier creams nearby in the beauty parlour. Then they lay behind the canvas walls that the wind plumped and rattled. One young man had brought a sand–yacht and, keeping to the wet, firm swath of beach, he skimmed along it under the sail's wing.

Greg and Magdalen sat where the dunes fringed the sand; it was dry and warm, spiked with grass. Now that the moment had come to recount what had happened, sweat bloomed her skin and her nails impressed crescents into her palms. Yesterday when she had spoken her father's word for her she had been desperate but this was more terrible, to sit where people were spending their holiday, to hear them calling to one another while she explained.

'I'm not sure there's anything you can't guess,' she said to him. She was stammering. 'I mean, it's not a unique experience. I know that now; I didn't know when I was younger.'

And suddenly she was appalled at herself. She was on the point of telling a man she hardly knew – had met for the first time less than a week ago – telling this Greg about her father. Her father, who had shared her life for eighteen years, not a paltry three days. Her chest tightened at the treachery; her head ached. 'He wasn't all bad.' Her voice creaked. 'He was a marvellous father, except for that. He was the tops.' Under her eyelids the tears gathered; she held them fast, forced them to disperse. 'Everything was good at the start. Not a misery in sight.' If she could make Greg understand that, she might forgive herself for this betrayal. She protested, 'I have to be fair to my father. I loved him.

'I don't remember much of my childhood, my infancy, I mean, when my mother was still alive. I realise now I was terribly spoilt. Though my father was busy, he's in marketing, he didn't bring his work home. When he was there, he gave all his energy to us; and he was great fun. He used to go round the house singing and he'd rig up jokes and surprises. Mum and the housekeeper loved them. I called the housekeeper Auntie Joanna and this probably sounds awful but I loved her more than Mum. She was the one who looked after me; we had to have her because of Mum's illness, leukaemia, but I didn't know anything about that at the time. Joanna's described the surprises that Dad arranged and there's one I have a vague memory of: the house smothered in flowers and a waiter with a napkin over his wrist. Apparently, with the help of Joanna, my father had sent in a catering firm without Mum's knowing. It was her birthday. I suppose she was

183

too frail to go out. Dad did marvellous things for me as well. He had a pilot's licence and he hired a plane and took me up in it. I was far too young to appreciate that, of course, but it was very exciting. Something was always happening when he was around. He's hyperactive. Also, he's a high achiever, very competitive. But that's not all of him. He can be very gentle. I remember lying in bed, hot and wretched and crying because the sun was wedged on my stomach like a hot water bottle and was making me feel sick, and he drew the curtain and wiped my face and arms with something cold. Joanna said I was about two, ill with measles, and he spent a whole week-end sitting by my bed.'

Was that how it began? she wondered. She didn't know. She had no memory of his doing more than wipe away the sweat and change her night-dress. But nursing her, was it then that he discovered he wanted a different kind of contact? If so, it must have been some time before he allowed it. He had tried to resist. She remembered her father's pale face after she had told him about the foot-steps outside her bedroom. 'He had a conscience at the beginning,' she murmured. 'I'm sure of that.'

Greg did not dare make the comment that sprang to his tongue: When it got in the way, his conscience was easily thrown out.

Magdalen sensed that he was not persuaded and she continued to describe the father who had played with her, had bought her presents, had taught her nursery rhymes, had never talked down to her. Regarding her as sensible and intelligent, he had never censored knowledge on the

184

grounds that she was too small. 'He would talk to me about anything on earth, saying it didn't matter if I didn't grasp all of it, I would some day. One minute he'd be asking: "Can you guess why Joanna calls the clothes rack hanging from the ceiling in the kitchen a winter hedge?" and the next he'd say: "Come out to the garage; I believe there's a fault in the distributor; I'll show you how it works." Teachers used to comment on my general knowledge. I owed it to him.'

'Does that include changing a wheel?'

'That came later. I let him show me since I thought being able to do it might come in useful, but it was a chore. By then I wanted to spend as little time as possible in his company.' She had done what she could to be just to her father and not one detail was untrue. She had painted him golden but she could no longer ignore his other, black side. 'When I couldn't bear to be near him, I'd run away.'

'Did you always come up here?'

She nodded. 'I remember the first time very clearly. I can't put a date on it, but I know exactly why I did. I'd been sleeping at Gail's, and staying with her family was a revelation. It didn't happen in her home. Then, because it didn't, I got it into my head that I was the only one. By then, of course, I knew it was him, my father. At first I'd thought it was something sent by Mr Hustler.'

'Who was Mr Hustler?'

'Our gardener. Still is. He does other jobs as well, like bits of house maintenance, the drains and so forth.'

'Gawd! You have a gardener as well as a housekeeper?'

'My father would do the garden if he could fit it in. His energy's limitless. Anyway, I was terrified of Mr Hustler when I was a kid. He's a perfectionist in the garden and he resented my playing in it. He used to threaten dire punishments – the bogyman, vampires, goblins, monsters – anything he could put his tongue to. So, when it began, I decided it was Mr Hustler sending something. That's how I worked it out. I was very little.

'I'd forgotten the explanations I gave for it all. I'd forgotten I'd blamed Mr Hustler till I began to write it down. I did it like a fairy-tale, with a princess living in a castle. Gail thinks the room where I work at home is like a turret; the rest of the idea I got from you, as I said. Today, I shan't be able to say the story how I wrote it, not exactly. I'll keep to it when I can, though, to help you understand how I felt, and how the house and people seemed to me. Writing the story has helped me get the events clear and in the proper order, so I'll begin with Mr Hustler.'

After a time she said, 'I'm feeling thirsty.' A man had just passed them, a bag clanging on his arm. He stopped, hitched up his bathing trunks with a thumb and took a long draught from a can. 'Really thirsty,' she repeated.

'Didn't you buy some soft drinks?'

'I intended to.'

He unpacked the carrier bag. 'Found them. That's it, then: orange juice, coke, pork pies, tomatoes, apples. A picnic for two.'

'Doesn't it look ordinary?'

'Yes.' He understood what she meant. Compared with

the situation she was describing, the food and the place seemed so natural, a relief.

A kite dived above their heads; its string looped and writhed as a woman tried to control it. A baby strapped to her chest was spread out like a small swimming frog.

Three people, their gender obscured by wet suits, rose out of the dunes behind them, strode across the beach with surf boards at the ready and sloshed purposefully into the sea. When it was slapping against their chests they lifted their boards above their heads as if threatening to wallop the incoming breaker. One made an error of judgement, disappeared, partially surfaced, was shovelled down the wave's dip, and dumped.

'I'd have a go at surfing if I had a wet suit,' Greg remarked.

'And a board.'

'That, too.'

So they ate and chatted until Magdalen felt able to resume.

Greg was a good listener. He did not appear to grow tired; his eyes did not slide away. Occasionally he would interrupt when there was something; a name, a reference, that he wished her to explain but the rest of the time he was still, concentrating.

He had never been told anything so intimate. Had he been younger he might have been squeamish and closed his ears but today he rebuked himself with: How you feel is irrelevant; think what it's been like for her. All the same, often he had to force himself to listen. Knowing the simple fact was easier than hearing the details. 'I'm sorry,'

187

she said once, seeing his discomfort, 'but this isn't new to me and I've been thinking it through a lot these last few days.'

She always called him, my father, like a child obeying precepts to be respectful, but the man was an ogre, Greg decided, nothing less. Temperamentally he was not violent but if Lindsay Wilde had appeared at that moment he would have kicked the sex out of him and locked his hands round his throat. He said, 'I wish there was something I could do, Magdalen.'

'You're doing it. Listening. That's great.'

So the hours passed. They left the dunes and walked along the beach, discovered a path through meadows and sat where grass had been cut for hay and new stalks sprouted through. While always nearby there were people enjoying their holiday or farmers attending to crops. But these went unnoticed. Until the sounds lessened and were softened by twilight. Then, admitting their hunger, they ate supper in a farmhouse and only separated to go to their beds.

Eighteen

It was on the second morning in the farmhouse that Magdalen said, 'I'll have to phone Mrs Brook.'

'I was thinking about that.'

'I'm sorry.'

'It has to be done.'

'I didn't mean the phoning, having to get back in touch, I meant . . .'

He interrupted, 'I know what you meant.' He put down his breakfast cup, considered another piece of toast and rejected the idea. 'I'm just as sorry that it's nearly over.'

She thrust aside the hope that the reason was the same as hers and said quickly, 'I can hardly believe that. Either you've been driving me around while I slept or thought and remembered, or you've been chasing after me and getting punched up, or you've had your ears bent by me yapping on.'

He smiled. 'It sounds as if I'm due for a putty medal, as my dad would say.'

'It's been all me.'

'It's done me good to have to listen. I'm always accused of being a garrulous bloke.'

'How long shall you stay at Melanie's?'

'Till the end of the month.'

Another week. Why couldn't she say: When we get home, let's go to the baths/listen to records/fetch a take-away/sit in a pub? Why couldn't she say: When we get home, won't you come round one evening?

She repeated, 'I'll have to ring Mrs Brook. See if there's anything from Edinburgh.'

Watching her leave the table, Greg thought: Didn't Ross say he's moving to Leith? That's close. I'll drop him a line. He'd put me up when term's started and she's settled. But watch it, Howkins, don't wait too long or some aspiring medico clutching his Gray's Anatomy and flashing a stethoscope will pip you to the post. Mustn't let that happen.

It had been dreadful listening to her. At first he didn't want to believe her; he didn't want to accept that it could have happened as she described. He wanted to protest, 'He can't have behaved like that; no one could, no one with his standing, with everyone's respect, with his civilised life style.' He wanted to deny that such things were possible, otherwise everything he cherished was turned upside down. And all the time he was certain that what he was hearing was true. Greg went through horror at the situation, nausea at the detail, fury that a father should persist in such selfish indulgence and found himself aching with distress. This was made worse because throughout Magdalen's voice remained even; it never rose to accuse. It was as if she were reciting a lesson or making a clinical report. There were occasions when he could bear this no longer and, muttering the need for a pee, he left her, stood apart in the dunes and spurted the tears which she did not shed. Once when he returned to her, she had observed: 'You must think I'm revolting,' and he had wanted to take her in his arms and rock her against his chest but instinct told him that, immersed in her history, she would shrink from him. The arms she felt round her would not be his. Therefore he had answered, 'No, I don't. I think exactly the opposite.' She had regarded him, puzzled; then timorous, had looked away, but she had remarked, 'You haven't heard everything yet.'

'It won't change what I've said,' he began but she had cut through his words and returned to her account.

As he sat in the farmhouse, after a sleep cracked by dreams, Greg said to himself, 'It's got to me, but I'll have to put up with that. Because she's got to me, too.'

Telephoning Mrs Brook, Magdalen asked whether any letter for her had arrived.

'I went up to the house early this morning to look at the post. There were some cards for you, but nothing came today with the Edinburgh post-mark. It'll be there tomorrow, though; that's promised. I've some good news, my dear. Your accommodation's arranged.'

'Marvellous.' She wanted to cartwheel over the doorstep, leapfrog the sun-dial, race across the field and jump the five-bar gate. 'How do you know?'

'Miss Howkins dropped in while I was there yesterday and we had a long talk. She was worried that the Allocations office of Accommodation Services – I think I've got that right – might not have picked up the message she left on the answering machine. So she gave them a ring, the staff were in the office by that time. And the upshot was, they put you in a hall of residence. All that's needed is for you to fill in the forms.'

'I'm so glad.'

'We are, too. You should have heard Miss Howkins. She can talk! She told them that since you were on holiday you couldn't submit an application at the moment, it would have been done before now except that there'd been an oversight at the school leading to you not being properly informed. She asked to speak to the one at the top. When she came off the phone she said, "I've never leant on anyone in that way before, Mrs Brook." I told her it was in a good cause and we had a little celebration. I fetched some glasses but I didn't want her to think I made a habit of that, so I explained, "I've not stolen Mr Wilde's sherry ever before." After she'd heard whose it was, she said we should have another, so we did.'

This scene of merrymaking shed new light on the two of them and Magdalen put a hand over the mouthpiece while she laughed.

'It was those two sherries, and I wouldn't swear there wasn't a third, that set me off.' Mrs Brook had reached a difficult moment and her voice faltered but, a woman with a conscience, she soldiered on. 'Like I said to Will, it wasn't me, it was the drink talking, and before I knew where I was, there I was making insinuations about Mr Wilde.'

She paused, waiting for a response but Magdalen was thinking: They were talking about Dad; they were talking about me. And him. Together. Her fears were translated into reality and despite her respect for the two women, she thought she could hear their exclamations of shock followed by gratified titillation; she imagined their faces flushed with curiosity or prurience, then the nods and complacent whispers: *You could see they were close.* She could picture them working out the details.

Sensing some of this, Mrs Brook said quickly, 'I didn't say anything to Miss Howkins that you wouldn't have wanted. I told her your father wouldn't be helping himself to a glass of sherry or anything else for that matter if there was any justice in this world. He'd be where I'd like to put him.'

'Where's that?' There was a sour taste in her mouth.

'Behind bars.'

Magdalen winced. Mrs Brook claimed she had said nothing that Magdalen wouldn't have wanted. Did she want that? The thought horrified her. She held the telephone in both hands to steady her grasp. 'Did you say that to Miss Howkins?' she whispered.

'I did indeed but as it turned out there wasn't any necessity. She'd guessed.'

'Guessed?' She could not believe it. 'When?'

'After what happened at the Moor Garage on Saturday morning. That grieved me, Magdalen. Why did you do it? Why couldn't you come to me?'

She could not say: I couldn't go to anyone. I couldn't go to you any more than I could go to anyone else. All she could manage was: 'I didn't dare.'

'Why ever should you be afraid of coming to me?'

'It's Dad I was afraid of.'

'I shouldn't have asked. It's not a subject to be talked about on the phone. But you might want to, some day?'

'Perhaps.'

'I'll be here if you do. All that's passed now, I hope, wanting to put an end to yourself?'

'Yes.'

'That's a great relief. I take a lot of the blame.'

'I don't know why you say that, Mrs Brook. It was me that decided on it.'

'I should never have let it get to that point. That cousin of Miss Howkins has earned my everlasting thanks. I hope that having him there you'll get it all off your chest.'

Magdalen almost answered: You make it sound as if I'm simply mentioning flat feet or flabby buttocks or worms. 'I'm trying.'

'That's the style. Now, when shall I expect you back?'

'I suppose we'd better drive home straight away.'

'There'll be no more post till tomorrow. Will's here signalling that Zeph Hustler . . .'

Zeph. Zephaniah. She'd never heard his first name.

'. . . has just passed by to say there's nothing in the second delivery . . .'

Miss Howkins, Mrs Brook, Mr Brook. Now Mr Hustler. How many of them were volunteering help?

'. . . so you aren't obliged to set off this minute. If you're enjoying yourself, why not stay through till tomorrow morning? You'd be back in time to see to the form and get it in the evening collection.'

194

'I'll do that.' This arrangement allowed one last day with Greg.

'In that case, I'll give your friend Gail a ring. I told her I would as soon as I had any news. She's been on the phone several times.'

'Why?'

'You'd gone on holiday, so I was told, hadn't you? You'd not mentioned that was on the cards. She didn't know what to make of it.'

'What did you tell her?' The trembling had returned. Why didn't she slam down the phone and run?

'I told her you'd gone off on an impulse. If you're asking, did I mention the business of your father, the answer's no, Magdalen.' The other sounded affronted. 'She's been your friend all the time I've worked for your family and years before that. If anything's said to her, it shouldn't come from me.'

'No.' Must she tell Gail? Lindsay Wilde had been her hero. As a child she had adored him. Later she would add, 'From afar.' That was when she had accepted her dreams were impossible, when she had stopped saying to Magdalen, 'I suppose you'll have to call me Mother after I've married him, but I won't mind if you forget.' Could she destroy such long-held illusions? Was it necessary to do that? Then Magdalen thought: But perhaps Gail would be equally desolated if she found that other people knew and she didn't. It's forced a gap between us for years. Despite the distress, might not Gail want to know?

Her silence renewed Mrs Brook's guilt. 'When I remarked on your father to Miss Howkins I was, in a manner of speaking, just letting her know that her theory was right.'

'Don't worry about it, Mrs Brook.'

'It just came out.'

'Helped by the sherry of course,' Magdalen reminded her and was pleased to hear the woman's relieved laugh.

'I'll see you tomorrow, then, my dear?'

'Yes, but hang on, don't go. There's something I've just thought of. I haven't my father's telephone number on me. Can you find it?'

'I don't need to look.' Without expressing surprise at the request she recited both Lindsay Wilde's office and hotel numbers while Magdalen wrote them down on the pad by the phone. She had no idea why she had asked for them but she slid the page into a pocket before she returned to Greg.

'That's great,' he said, when she had told him her news. 'As well as being safer, you'll enjoy living in Hall. And now you're suggesting we stay on another day?'

'If you'd like to.'

'You don't have to twist my arm. I was only wondering whether we need to go to a cash point again. Berwick's the nearest. How much have you got?'

Now they divided the money and took it in turns to pay.

'About twenty-eight pounds.'

'I've counted my little wad and after I've paid this morning I'll have fifteen pounds forty.'

'So we'll have enough for another bed and breakfast and petrol, plus a sandwich.'

'If we haven't, we can always trade our fixed assets as part payment.'

'Such as?'

'A couple of buckets and spades.'

'Worth about a litre of petrol. We might do better to offer our labour, sort of work our passage. I could service the farm machinery while you mucked out the cows.'

In this mood they threw the rucksack into the car and left the farmhouse, both happy at the prospect of another day together and Magdalen telling herself: It must be his.

Therefore when Greg reached the road and asked, 'Where shall we make for? Do we find another beach?' she answered, 'You choose.'

'Do you want to walk and talk or just laze around?' The sky was still cloudless; only the wind off the nearby sea tamed the heat of the sun.

'We've done what I wanted for two whole days. Now it's your turn.'

'Fair enough. There's somewhere I'd really like to go. All the places we've stayed at have had leaflets about it. I've swotted it up. Holy Island. Lindisfarne. Have you been?'

'No.' She was glad that he had such a ready suggestion. 'Not yet.'

'It's a few miles off the coast road.' He had paused at a T-junction and was examining the signpost. 'The trouble is, that for two chunks of the day you can't reach it, the tide cuts it off and it is, literally, an island. When the tide's out, you cross to it over a causeway.'

'I like the sound of that.'

'Yeah, it's good. Let's hope the tide's not in when we get there. If it is, we'll have something like a four-hour wait.'

Nineteen

They did not have to wait before crossing to Lindisfarne. When they drove through the strip of marsh grasses and halted on a bridge over a thin course of water, it was clear that the tide had receded. In the shallows below them black glossy weeds draped over pebbles and a redshank pecked. Further off, other birds bustled. Sensing their presence they rose suddenly in a flock, a dazzle of white chevrons on their wings. 'Oyster-catchers,' Greg told her. Then they continued along a road that was puddled with sea water and gritty with sand left by the last tide; until it became bordered by marsh, passed through rough tufted dunes, found grassland where sheep nibbled, and entered a small group of houses.

In the car park Greg hung the buckets from the straps of the rucksack and stuck the spades into the side pockets. They stood upright like makeshift aerials.

'Kit for the sand,' he told her. 'Today's play day and I'm in charge.'

They strolled into the village, discovered a shop, and Greg bought Vienna slices 'to jazz up the cattle cake' he said, referring to the packed lunch from the farm. He added ice-creams and asked her, 'How about a few bags of crisps?'

'I'm sure they'll come in handy.'

'One thing I like about you, Magdalen: you don't have diet fads.'

'After all this, I may have to start.'

They dawdled along the street absorbed in their ice-cream, their tongues grooming it into soft peaks and pursuing the drips, their teeth biting a pattern of scallops round the edge of the cone, their lips sucking the final drops through a hole in its point. They loitered past the sparse houses, considered the herring boats halved and inverted to make roomy sheds, admired the strong beam of the keel and the elegance of the fat, pear-shaped hull curving down to the grass, while the sun continued to warm them and the tide rose over the causeway sealing this finger of sand and rock from the rest of the land.

'Have you seen that?' Greg asked, pointing ahead.

'You can hardly miss it.'

Looking over the sway of the sea and the cropped level fields, was an abrupt concise tor. Grass covered its base but, as the slopes thrust up, they became harsh rock. It was precisely capped without margin by low towers and sturdy plain walls.

Greg said, 'Do you see the lines of strata showing through the grass and going round? They make it look like a walnut whirl.'

'Yes, it does!'

'Shall we go in?' People were straggling up the path which curled round the crag. 'I've read about it. It's open in the afternoon.'

'But you've brought the buckets and spades.'

'There's plenty of time. We can't leave even if we wanted to because the causeway's closed till nearly five. The timetable was in the shop. After that, it's open again till half after midnight. We can look for some sand when the tide's out.'

'I'm not sure that I fancy a castle.'

'This was never much of one, just a small fort for defending the coast. It's been reconstructed. The owner lived in it up to twenty or thirty years ago. It was more of a home than a castle. I'd like to look at it.'

So she agreed, reminding herself: This is Greg's day.

Walking by his side, Magdalen could feel him close to her; their arms brushed, their feet moved in step. And suddenly she wished he would take her hand. She wished he would say: Look, don't let's bother with the castle; let's go and find somewhere that's private; but the thought was hardly completed before she was shrinking away. As she always had done, with other young men. She remembered how she would adopt complicated manoeuvres to avoid an arm round her waist, a kiss; recalled the hurt on the decent, puzzled face. Then she would be remorseful, would contrive a swift hug and a frivolous peck before her skin conquered and she could not suppress its flinch of revulsion or breathe the air plugged in her throat.

They followed the other visitors climbing the path, then up a long cobbled ramp. At the entrance, they found a man, index finger retaining his place in the guidebook while he studied the lintel over the door. 'There it is, the portcullis,' he told them, eager to inform the ignorant. 'It's operated by winding gear and weights in the scullery that's situated directly above.'

'Thanks for mentioning it,' Greg said. 'I'll dodge out of the way if it comes down. I don't want to end up impaled.'

'It's not used any more. It's just kept as a feature,' the man explained, conscientious.

'I see. What about the drawbridge? My friend has a special interest in them.'

'You don't have a drawbridge without a moat.' Then the man threatened, 'Just watch it!' and strode off.

Greg smiled at her. 'Heard what he said? I told you it's not at all like a regular castle.'

When they had paid their fee and were wandering around, he demanded, 'Can you imagine anything sinister going on in this kitchen? I can't. For that matter, I can't imagine much cooking going on either. Where did they fry the chips? It's too comfortable. Look at that settle! Just the right shape for a nap.'

Magdalen stood at a window and looked at the sluicing sea while he chatted to a guide.

'There aren't any dungeons,' he reported and led her through the hall and down steps. 'Nothing lower than this.' They stood in the dining room. Steeply vaulted and narrow, it was surprisingly domestic and snug.

'It's like something out of the tales of King Arthur,' she commented.

'You're right; it is.'

'Except that the table isn't round.'

'You can't have everything. The whole atmosphere's

very romantic. All the same, I can't quite picture a stately damsel wearing a hennin when you're standing there in jeans.'

Magdalen thought: Would Gail have tried to keep his attention focused on the jeans? Saying, My mum thinks they're too tight. Then probably swaying down the room like a model on a cat-walk. Quickly she asked Greg, 'What's a hennin?'

'A funnel-shaped hat with a veil hanging from the point.'

'I know the kind you mean.'

I'm stupid, Magdalen thought. Why do I have to make everything so heavy for myself? Why can't I be normal? That comment on my jeans meant nothing. It had no significance. It wasn't a try, a pass. It wasn't even a compliment particularly, or a kind of teasing. Why, as soon as there's a hint of anything personal, can't I handle it? I'm like a kid, so unsophisticated it's not true.

Standing in that simple, elegant room she felt awkward with him, gauche. Laboriously, she told him, 'I haven't come across the word "hennin" before.'

'I've read a bit on costume.'

He had turned and was examining the side table. They had left the rucksack with the attendant in the entrance hall; where its straps had been, his T-shirt was marked by patches of sweat. She saw his back flinch as if his shoulder blades itched, and she recalled her sleepless night waiting for the results. She had wanted to scratch her back and she had thought her father would know the word for that section of it that was difficult to reach.

'What's the word for the part of your back that's hard to get at?' she asked Greg.

'No idea.' He was absorbed in scrutinising the design of a pewter tankard.

'Perhaps there isn't such a word,' she murmured. Perhaps she had imagined the word existed, and so naturally she had told herself that her father would know it. It was time she broke this childish habit of believing that he is a polymath, an expert on everything. She smiled at Greg's back as he preceded her along the passage and up a flight of stairs, wanting to say to him: If you ever do come across the word, you needn't tell me what it is.

'This is better than I'd hoped,' he said. They were standing in a long gallery, the floor striped by the sun. 'Do you like it?'

'I like it very much.'

'I think I'll do a sketch. But let's have a look at the bedrooms first.'

He was stepping towards a door but was halted by a voice which called, stentorian, 'Turn right.' It came from a woman sitting behind an oak table on which were lined up leaflets, National Trust information and maps. She was wearing a jacket reminiscent of a horse blanket and her hair and hat were neatly squared off. 'East bedroom first,' she ordered.

'Sorry, I didn't quite catch,' Greg called back, and did not alter direction. Laughing, they stood behind the door while the gallery they had left echoed with outrage and fog-horn rebukes.

'She's probably got her finger jammed on the panic button,' he whispered.

'You're a marked man, now. She'll ban the sketchbook.'

The room they were in was small and uncluttered, the furniture handsome.

'It's so pretty,' she said.

'Yes.' His expression had become serious. Delicately he flicked a dandelion seed off her sleeve. 'See, not a cobweb, Magdalen. I bet there's not a single skeleton or ghost. The only monster is that witch out there.'

She watched the seed glide in the draught of his speaking and kept her eyes upon it as it dived down, rolled frail but vigorous across the carpet and came to rest on the floor. That was painted a deep green, a Lutyens colour. She wanted to tell him: I know why you persuaded me to come here, Greg. I know why you hoped I'd like it, and what you're saying this castle proves. You're saying: A castle isn't always a fortress. It doesn't always have secrets to guard. These walls are thick and seal off all sounds, but their windows do not let in the odour of roses, only the light that dazzles from the vast sea. You are telling me: It is possible for a princess to live in a castle and to find that she is not a prisoner; it is possible for her to be free of terrors and disgust. But I want you to understand, Greg, that I no longer fear it. When I return to my castle I shall not be its prisoner. I can escape. Escape is not to run away or live somewhere else – that is easy. It is to overcome the power of the memories and all that my castle contained. And I wish you to know that I can do that now, Greg. Because of you.

She could feel the tears hot under her eyelids. She wanted to reach to him and stroke his cheeks. She wanted to say: Thank you for listening, for believing, for not pushing. She wanted to say: You're a lovely man. But the words would not come.

Then the castle she had described and the things that had been done in it and her hand that could not lift to Greg's face were meshed together. The anger bud that had been waiting within her stretched and strained. And at last it burst open. She stood in the middle of that bedroom and shouted, 'The bastard! He's a bastard! He's fouled me up!'

Before a loud voice was ordering her to leave the castle that minute, she heard another, quieter and relieved. It said, 'I'm glad you've said that, Magdalen.'

Twenty

She was running along the passage, jumping down steps and under the portcullis, was hurtling down the cobbled ramp and racing across grass. While behind her Greg offered excuses to placate the attendant she had pushed out of her way. Then she was clattering over pebbles, sliding on stones.

The shore was not like the one she had fled to three days earlier. She did not paddle through shallows and the waves' glittering foam. No pools held the reflection of clouds or breathed up a promise in her mother's comforting voice. There was no sand for her to leap and dance upon, where she could draw pictures whose obscenity was cleansed by the waves. She had not come here to seek consolation. She had come to rage.

Now by the water's edge she kicked at pebbles, clawed them up and flung them into the sea. She grabbed seaweed, dragged it in great skeins and beat with it, flailing the rocks. She tore through sea-wrack, heaved up broken timber, swung it to spin and crash. She stamped on an empty can, crushed it, hurled it into the waves. Stumbling over metal, she levered it up, drove it, a brine-rusted stake, into the stone-covered ground. Shrieking at her father: It's you that stops me. Wildly her body lunged, her fists punched and her knees jabbed. And she was running again, shouting: It's you that makes me cringe away; it's you holds me back. You're there always, pressing the buttons. Until, exhausted, her blood pounding, her legs buckling, she tripped and slithered, went down upon barnacles and a litter of shells.

Stretched out, her legs bruised, her lungs screaming for air, she heard another's throat grate, saw a rucksack dropped and Greg squat, lean on it for support. Neither had the breath to speak.

But finally she panted, 'I used to shy away from them, boys I went out with. I wouldn't kiss them. I used to wince if they touched.'

Her hands scratched at a rib of rock. 'I'd call a halt the moment anyone tried to make a pass. I got myself to believe I did that because I didn't like them enough, not enough to let them . . .

'That was a lie. There were one or two I went for, one or two I imagined myself going out with, properly, I mean, but I could never bring myself to accept them. I'd find a reason, blame it on them.

'But they had nothing to do with it. It was him, my father.' She was crouching now, grinding pebbles in a clenched fist.

'I'd tell them my father would be waiting up, or wandering around. I didn't stop to consider the irony of that – me using Dad to get rid of them, using him as a protection when it was his fault! It wasn't the boys I needed protection from. It was Dad.

'The way I was feeling wasn't because of what they wanted, it wasn't because they wanted to kiss me or embrace. When I felt my skin rise in goose-pimples it was because it couldn't do anything else. Not after years with my father.'

Abruptly she tossed the pebbles away. 'Greg, the way I felt about the others, it's been the same with you.'

'It wasn't something you could hide.'

'I'm very sorry. It's not that, somehow, I don't want . . . There have been times.' She remembered, after their fight, when she had finally uttered her father's word for her, she had been glad that his fingers remained on her wrist. 'I don't know. I'm muddled.'

'That's not your fault.'

'It's so stupid.'

'No, it's not.'

'I can't control it.'

'That won't last.'

'But, how long?' She raised her head and gave a high, piercing wail: 'How long?' Eerie, the sound rode on the wind and was caught in the lifting sea.

Greg eased himself upright. 'Let's move from here. We need bum shields against these stones.'

Slowly they walked over the fields in the direction of the castle 'It's his fault,' her voice clanged. 'He's made me like this. I don't know what it is to feel natural. Spontaneous.'

'You will.'

'And how?' she demanded, harsh, bitter.

'You'll find a way.'

'Shall I?' For a time she was silent.

'It's always me left with the problem. That's the difference. The difference between him and me. For years he does what he likes and I have to . . .' The muscles in her cheeks pulsed. 'I have to put up with it. No matter what it does to me. When it's over, it'll be me left to cope while he walks away, not a care in the world. Just like it's always been. He won't have any of the miseries or nightmares or hang-ups. When it's over, all that'll bother him is, his pride will be hurt.'

Greg did not agree with her. He considered that without his daughter Lindsay Wilde would be lost. He was dependent upon her and would feel bereaved. But Greg did not say this. It was the wrong moment. She might think he suggested that the man deserved sympathy. It was more important to ensure that she could make the break. 'You said, when it's over. Do you really mean that?'

'Yes.'

'Good.'

'Will that make me a changed person?'

'I hope not in every respect.'

'I told Gail I was going to reinvent myself, ready for Edinburgh, starting with a haircut; but I didn't imagine making a complete break with Dad. I was just concentrating on being free of him, and I thought I should be, if I got up there. That wasn't very bright of me. Having a place to live is a great help, but what about the vacs? And why should I hide? So I'm going to settle him once and for all.'

Greg stopped. 'Say that again.'

'I'm going to settle him once and for all.'

'Brilliant! Now, you see those people standing on the lower battery?' He pointed up to the castle. 'We'll yell it to them.'

'Like they say people who want to give up smoking should tell everyone, then they will? I shall do what I've decided without that.' But she shouted with him until they ran out of breath.

'I'd like to do that when he's there,' she told him. 'I'd like to catch him when he's surrounded by everyone at home that knows him: Mr Gresham and the rest of the staff at school, and Mrs Dawson across the road and Mrs Brook and Mr Brook and Zephaniah Hustler and all his mates at the golf club and the manager at the Moor Garage.' Anger had given place to revenge. She stood with her head back, taking the wind, no longer afraid that people would think her disgusting. 'I'd wait till there was a lull in the conversation then I'd say, raising my voice just enough for them all to hear, I'd say: "Let me introduce you to Lindsay Wilde the rapist who has used me incestuously for fifteen years." That'd cause a stir! It'd take all his charm to pass that off!

'Or what do you think about a bit of torture? It doesn't rule out the other, of course. I could do both. For the torture I could send him letters, anonymously, on the lines of: If you don't stop what you are doing, your friends and acquaintances, your staff and the other directors will be told what you are.'

'I'm not fond of blackmail.'

'I could send letters to the secretaries of his clubs, tell them.'

'I expect he could argue himself out of that.'

'Yes. The more straightforward approach is better. For one thing, I'd see his face and, if I made the announcement in public, I wouldn't be obliged to repeat it to people separately. I could walk into one of his top level conferences, and just as he was about to speak, interrupt and say, "I'm here to give you the true facts about this man".'

'I reckon you'd be thrown out.'

'I could murder him. I really could.' Her eyes were on the profile of a ship on the horizon, its movement barely perceptible. Her expression was fixed and intent.

Greg told her hurriedly, 'I'd forget that. I mean, how old is he?'

Surprised, she had to relinquish other thoughts to calculate. 'Forty-seven. No, forty-eight.'

Greg pursed his lips, pretending to make an estimation. 'He's in a high-risk age bracket: coronaries, hypertension, alcohol poisoning. Flat feet. Worms. He'll snuff it first.'

'I'm not joking, Greg.'

'Just testing. After the last couple of days I was worried I might've lost the gift. Come on, Magdalen. Don't be uptight. Don't frown.'

'It's something you said. It rang a bell. I know.' Her face smoothed. 'This morning, on the phone, Mrs Brook made telling you about my father sound the same as saying I'd got flat feet or worms. That's what I thought. You used the same words. Isn't that weird?'

'Great minds.'

She smiled. 'I added something else, though, that you didn't mention.'

'Yes?'

'Drooping buttocks.'

'Those, too? I'd resigned myself to flat feet and worms as part of the job lot. But droopy buttocks! Glad you've mentioned them. They really turn me on.'

They had come to the beach again and as they stepped down the slope, avoiding the stubs of white rock half hidden in the grass, he put out his hand. She took it and jumped down. It was a simple, commonplace movement, and not until she had released his hand and was regarding the building in front of them did she realise what she had done. This isn't the moment to cry, she warned herself sharply; crying at something *good*.

She asked, 'What's this? Do you know?'

'It's a kiln. The guide mentioned it. They used to quarry for limestone the other end of the island and fire it in this. Ships taking out the lime would moor up here; there was a jetty, apparently.'

'I've never seen one so big.' It was high, built of stone. Fragments of quartz glittered in the sun. 'It makes kilns in the Dales look miniscule.'

'There's more than one oven. I suppose that's why they needed the entrances.' There were three of them, each spanned by a neat rounded arch. Along the next wall they could see four others; the vault of one was pointed. 'Was this the main entrance, do you think?' she asked.

He followed her inside, pleased by her absorption,

saying to himself: Nice she's calmed down, after all the rumpus; something came out of it, though: she vowed she would settle her father once and for all. Shouted it. But how's she going to do that? And when?

However, he felt certain that he must not interfere. Reluctantly he reminded himself: She must take her own time.

Closed against the afternoon brilliance, the kiln was dark, a brown colour which rose from the floor's muddied sand. He was in a passage wide enough for a cart and ceilinged with brick. Ahead of him the darkness was slightly diffused and, stepping a few yards, Greg discovered that the passage he was in was crossed by another; at its end a stubby archway framed the beach and the sea. He understood that these lanes formed a grid; within their walls were the ovens. Flues and troughs burrowed into their base. There was no sign of Magdalen.

It was cold in the kiln. The wind crept down the passageways and siffled in the flues. It must have been sweltering in here, Greg said to himself, when the ovens were banked up. He imagined the vermilion coals, the flare of the flames, the smoke spouting and the incandescent lime. I expect it reeked, too, he added. Today its smell was no more wholesome. Its corners were fetid; its walls held the customary odours of neglect. Suddenly Greg was anxious. He walked into the next passage and his were the only feet making a sound. He called, 'Magdalen,' but there was no answer. He wanted her with him; he wanted her by his side; he wanted to stride out of this place with her, leave its smell and its coldness behind them and stroll in the burning sun; he wanted to hold her; he wanted to feel her skin bare and warm against his.

Searching, he ran down the cartways, stumbled in the bulging dark and peered. Until a shaft of light brought him to bricks where the wall had collapsed, opening the great belly of an oven. It rose to a wide vent covered with a grating of iron. Above was a circle of sky. Magdalen was crouched in the dust at the bottom of the oven, her hands over her face.

'Mrs Brook says he ought to be behind bars,' she whispered.

He agreed with her but he could not say it. Gentle, he picked out a small feather caught in her hair.

'I can't do it. I can't do that to him. I can't get him locked up. For him, that would be worse than murder.' She raised her head. Her eyelids were rashed; the shadows falling from the iron grille chequered her shoulders and cheeks. 'Whatever else he is, he remains my father. Must I take revenge? Do that to him?'

The question was not directed to Greg. It was not for him to answer.

After a time, she murmured, 'I know what you're thinking.'

He shook his head.

'Yes. You're thinking: There could be others; they must be protected.'

He could not deny it.

'I could warn him. I could say that if I suspected it, I should report him. Blackmail, I suppose,' she answered, weary. 'But it would be a technicality. It wouldn't be needed. There won't be others. I'm sure of that. He's not a paedophile. There was only ever me.'

His chest heaved at her grieving, but she had not said: There *is* only me, and his mind rejoiced at her *was*.

Again she told him, 'I know what you're thinking.' Then, later, 'I've got his telephone numbers.'

Slowly she pushed her legs out of the oven, uncurled and slid into the passage. Upright, she asked, 'What time is it?' She grasped his arm, brought it into the light and scrutinised his watch, oblivious of the one on her own wrist. 'He won't have left the office yet. I'll phone there.'

Apprehensive, Greg nodded. The mile back to the village was the longest he had ever walked.

In the post office as he dialled he tried to shield her from the attention of the postmistress. A voice on the line repeated the number. 'One moment, please,' he was told; 'I'll switch you through.'

Magdalen took the handset. He had never seen such anguish on a face. 'Sit on this,' he coaxed and dragged up a stool.

She was saying, 'May I speak to Mr Wilde?'

The voice answered, 'He's in a meeting. Can I take a message? Or would you like me to ring you back?'

'I wish to speak to him.'

The voice continued, polite, 'Who is it, please?' and at her answer, requested, 'Would you please hold?' The words were hurried; the tone hinted excitement.

Immediately, contradicting his secretary's excuse, Lindsay Wilde spoke. 'Magdalen! My dear. I've been out of my mind with worry. Where are you speaking from?'

Greg heard: 'I haven't rung you to talk, Dad. There's something I have to say and I want you to listen.' Then he walked to the counter and did not dare look back. As he tried to distract himself and the postmistress with an inconsequential patter, he had the sense that his speech was disordered, that the words crackled on his dry tongue. Staring at the woman, he did not see her; the image before him was Magdalen's face, the lips whitening, the chin rapped by the shaking phone. At the sight, his own hands trembled.

But Magdalen was not long speaking to her father. There was the click of the telephone, her swift steps, and they were standing on the pavement. She was talking: 'I used to dream of doing it. But I daren't. I used to swear: One day I'll yell, Keep away from me.' She was hunched, her voice muffled; it was difficult for him to hear. 'One day, I'll get the upper hand. One day I shall win. One day I shall have the victory. Well, now I have.'

He thought: I ought to be saying, That's great. I ought to be congratulating her on being firm and tough. But he could see no exhilaration. She was not smiling. She was not deafening him with a jubilant: I've settled him now, once and for all.

She was moaning, 'He just caved in. He cried. He said he was ashamed. He said he'd often wished that something would happen to prevent it.'

She paused; the words were borne on the swell of approaching tears. 'He could have been stopped sooner. If something had happened to prevent it. Do you hear that,

Greg? If something had happened. If someone had found out. If I'd said what I've said to him today. He might have been stopped sooner. But nobody knew it was happening. And I didn't think I could make it stop. I could only imagine telling him. I didn't believe it was possible, that it could be done. Do you understand, Greg? I might have put an end to it long before now. It might have been finished long, long ago.'

Then her face crumbled and at last the tears gushed. He stretched out and she came to him, was held in the hoop of his arms and he caressed her, murmuring comfort, stroked the tears on her cheeks knowing his own were wet. Supporting her, taking her weight, he led her along the pavement and out of the village.

At the car he wrapped her in the rug and helped her inside. He opened the boot and threw in the rucksack that only that morning he had trimmed with buckets and spades. They remained shiny and dry. Another time, he thought, we'll play with them. Perhaps, next summer, we will celebrate this day. He guessed that ahead of them the months would not be easy; there was still much for them to acknowledge and accept.

He started the engine, drove out of the car park and on to the causeway. Since their arrival, it had been covered but once more the sea had drawn back, the waves kept their distance and Lindisfarne was joined again to the land. As he had done that morning, Greg halted on the bridge. They looked at the stream under them, then behind them, the dunes. 'Home next,' he said. 'We have to go back sometime.'

'Yes, and now I don't mind.' The warmth of the rug had stilled her shaking. For the first time since she was a child, Magdalen did not wince as she sensed the soft graze of a man's lips. And reaching for his hand, she nuzzled against him, secure in affection and trust.